"Do you need anything from me before—" Alex asked.

Joanna shook h[er head.]
Unable to resist [... her]
hair, his fingers [...]
tresses. "I do."

Joanna realized she was hardly breathing. "What do you need?"

"You." His gaze went to the soft lock of her hair he was winding around his finger. "I didn't realize it would be so difficult to sleep with you in the next room. I wanted you beside me with your hair spread out on the pillow, your body next to mine."

A faint smile curved her mouth, a glimmer of excitement flickered in her eyes. "I'm here now," she said softly.

He sank down on the bed, pulling her with him and wrapping her in his arms. His hands caressed the bare skin of her arms, then slid her nightgown up to bare her thigh.

Joanna closed her eyes. She shouldn't be here. She shouldn't be enjoying his hands on her body. She shouldn't be responding to the hunger in his eyes and the heat in his caress.

Then he spoke, his voice low and raw with longing. "Touch me. . . ."

WHAT ARE *LOVESWEPT* ROMANCES?

They are stories of true romance and touching emotion. We believe those two very important ingredients are constants in our highly sensual and very believable stories in the *LOVESWEPT* line. Our goal is to give you, the reader, stories of consistently high quality that may sometimes make you laugh, sometimes make you cry, but are always fresh and creative and contain many delightful surprises within their pages.

Most romance fans read an enormous number of books. Those they truly love, they keep. Others may be traded with friends and soon forgotten. We hope that each *LOVESWEPT* romance will be a treasure—a "keeper." We will always try to publish

*LOVE STORIES YOU'LL NEVER FORGET
BY AUTHORS YOU'LL ALWAYS REMEMBER*

The Editors

LOVESWEPT® • 311

Patt Bucheister
Near the Edge

BANTAM BOOKS
TORONTO • NEW YORK • LONDON • SYDNEY • AUCKLAND

NEAR THE EDGE
A Bantam Book / February 1989

If you would be interested in receiving protective vinyl
covers for your Loveswept books, please write to this address
for information:

Loveswept
Bantam Books
P.O. Box 985
Hicksville, NY 11802

ISBN 0-553-21962-6

Published simultaneously in the United States and Canada

Bantam Books are published by Bantam Books, a division
of Bantam Doubleday Dell Publishing Group, Inc. Its
trademark, consisting of the words "Bantam Books" and
the portrayal of a rooster, is Registered in U.S. Patent and
Trademark Office and in other countries. Marca Registrada.
Bantam Books, 666 Fifth Avenue, New York, New York 10103.

PRINTED IN THE UNITED STATES OF AMERICA

O   0 9 8 7 6 5 4 3 2 1

One

The sound of a man yelping in pain was as startling and unexpected as a whip cracking in a public library.

All conversation stopped briefly in the room and all heads turned to see what caused the unusual commotion. A man was holding his foot awkwardly, staring at a woman. She was glaring back at him, her hands planted on her hips.

This was all very exciting for the inhabitants of Chesham, who were attending an art exhibit in the Whitehill Community Centre. The exhibit was an event for the small village in Buckinghamshire County in England. But at the moment, the paintings and their artists took second place as the main attraction. It was rare to see a woman stomp on a man's foot in public, and it was worth a few minutes of their attention.

Conversations resumed gradually, although curious glances slid toward the man limping out of the center and the woman who had attacked his foot. Many of the townspeople recognized the woman as the American granddaughter of a longtime resident, but the man was a complete stranger.

If asked, the general consensus of the citizens of Chesham would be that Americans were a curious lot and could be counted on to make an occasion interesting.

Most people began studying the paintings again. Alex Tanner, however, continued staring at the dark-haired woman.

"I hope your opening line is better than that chap's," the Englishman next to him said.

Alex barely heard. He was concentrating on the woman. Her expression revealed her fury, but he noticed she didn't take the easy way out, leaving the room as the embarrassed man had.

"I thought you said she was shy," Alex murmured.

Richard Sanders clarified his statement. "I said she was quiet and self-contained."

The woman walked toward the buffet table. "Tell me the rest," Alex ordered.

"She's twenty-five, educated at Stanford University in California. Mother deceased. Father is Franklyn Kerr, United States senator, who resides in Washington, D.C. There's a younger brother, Travis, age twenty, college student. She lives in Seattle, Washington, where she works as a speech therapist. Her reason for being in England is to visit her maternal grandmother, Elizabeth Montain, which she does once a year. She usually comes in July, but for some reason she chose to come in March this year. So far, we haven't discovered what that reason was.

She suddenly asked for three week's leave from the clinic where she works and arranged for someone else to take over her clients."

Without taking his gaze off the woman, who was now helping herself to some canapés, Alex asked, "What about her private life?"

"There's not much. You didn't give us a lot of time on this, you know. The report from Seattle states that she pays her rent on time and stays pretty much to herself. The administrator of the clinic she works for has high praise for her professionalism. She keeps a low profile as the senator's daughter. In fact, the people she works with aren't aware of who her father is. According to our government sources, she's refused any security arrangements, even though her father has requested it while he's involved in crime syndicate hearings."

The agent paused to collect his thoughts, then went on. "There's no lover that we could come up with. If there is one, she doesn't bring him to her apartment and no one can remember her being seen frequently with any one man. According to the agent in Seattle, her landlady would be the type to keep track of everyone coming and going in her apartments. Miss Kerr owns a late model car, nothing fancy, American-made. There's no police record. Not even a parking ticket. Joanna Kerr seems to lead a very dull life."

Dull wasn't one of the adjectives Alex would have chosen to describe Joanna Kerr. He examined the way her ivory knit dress flowed gently over the curves of her slender body. She looked cool and unapproachable, yet touchable, a contradiction he didn't understand but could recognize. The gentle slope of her hips and the provocative rise of her breasts were made for a man's hands. His own hands clenched, and he was startled to realize he wanted to touch her.

To get his thoughts away from her body, he forced his gaze up to her face. Her thick brown hair was pulled back at the nape of her neck by an ivory ribbon, exposing the clean lines of her jaw and accentuating her wide dark eyes.

At that instant, she raised her gaze and looked directly at him. She stared at him for a long moment, then frowned and turned away.

The black and white photograph he had seen in Washington D.C. didn't do her justice. His first impression as he had examined the photo was of a reasonably attractive woman with dark hair and dark eyes, smiling as if she didn't have a care in the world. He saw now an unsmiling woman with shadows in her eyes. Of course, her expression could be because of the scene with that man, but Alex didn't think so. If she had been upset by the incident, she would have left.

After observing her for the last half hour, he realized the impression Senator Kerr had given him was as flat as that one-dimensional photo. There had been no indication of the innate sensuality in her every move. In person she was a vital, alluring woman who only had to walk across the room to draw men's eyes to her long legs and slim hips. Amazingly enough, she didn't seem to be aware of it, or if she was, she didn't take advantage of it.

She bit into a petite sausage roll. Alex felt a slash of heat cut into his body as her tongue slowly stroked across her bottom lip. He took turns silently cursing his reaction and cursing her father, who was responsible for him being in England. Lusting after the senator's daughter was not part of the deal.

Her lithe grace stirred his imagination as she strolled from the buffet table to one of the paintings. Thoughts of her legs entangled with his and her dark hair spread over his shoulders and chest hardened his body. Damn, he didn't like the immediate attraction he felt for her. In fact, he didn't like anything about this assignment. If anyone else but Senator Kerr had asked him, he would never have come out of early retirement to take this case.

The voice of the man next to him startled him, but he kept his expression as impassive as ever. "So what's your next move, Alex?" Without waiting for an answer, Richard continued in his clipped British accent. "I would keep in mind she apparently doesn't take kindly to advances from strange men."

Alex ignored the Englishman's dry humor. "Who's the artist of the painting she's looking at?"

"I haven't the faintest idea." Richard handed Alex the catalogue he had received at the door. "This is the list of artists and paintings. It's an exhibit of local amateur painters who got together to show their work, so don't expect to dazzle her with your knowledge of the masters."

Alex took the catalogue and pushed away from the wall he had been leaning against. "I'll be in touch."

Richard chuckled. "Yes, I imagine you will. Just remember, she doesn't seem to be the type of woman who treads lightly, if you get my meaning."

Maneuvering easily between the groups of people cluttering the room, Alex approached Joanna Kerr.

She was standing alone in front of an abstract painting. For a couple of minutes he simply stood next to her and studied the same painting.

"What's it supposed to be?" he asked in a conversational tone.

Joanna turned her head in the direction of the man's voice, but had to raise her eyes in order to find his face. She recognized the man whose gaze had held hers briefly a few minutes ago. He was the type of man who would stand out in a crowd. It was more than just his height, which she guessed to be several inches over six feet. He wore a gray leather waist-length jacket over a white shirt. Charcoal-gray slacks accentuated his lean hips and tall frame. There was something vaguely familiar about him, but she didn't know what. One thing she did know was that she had never met him before. She would have remembered.

He was looking down at her, and she realized he had been speaking to her. Hoping he was merely making polite conversation and not coming on to her, she replied, "It's supposed to be a boy fishing."

"Which blob is the boy?"

She turned back to the painting. "I haven't the faintest idea." Smiling, she added, "It's given me a whole new outlook on my grandmother's neighbor."

It was odd, she thought, how she knew he was looking at her and not the painting. She could feel his gaze as though it were actually touching her. She glanced at him, and saw his puzzled expression. "The artist is Mrs. Westbrook," she explained, "a very proper English gentlewoman who is horrified if the crusts are not properly trimmed off the watercress sandwiches. She makes her gardener use

a level on the top of her hedges when he trims
them." Pulling her gaze back to the painting, she
added, "I find it hard to believe she painted anything as undisciplined as this."

"You're an American."

She looked at him, allowing a touch of cool amusement to enter her eyes. "So are you."

He smiled. Holding out his right hand, he introduced himself. "I'm Alex Tanner. Houston, Texas."

That explained the slight drawl in his voice, she
mused. She took his hand briefly, then dropped her
own. The callouses on his palm and fingers indicated he didn't spend a great deal of time behind a
desk. There was also a waiting stillness about him,
as if he were a predatory animal ominously standing
guard.

Suddenly she realized why he seemed familiar.
She didn't recognize the man himself, but the type
of man he was struck a familiar chord in her mind.

"You're a long way from home, Mr. Tanner," she
said coolly.

"An introduction usually consists of both parties
giving their names," he said softly.

She continued to hold his gaze without giving
ground. "Is that how it's done in Houston?"

"I believe that's how it's done everywhere."

"Have you been everywhere?"

"Just about."

"I bet you have," she said dryly. It had been a
stupid question. Her gaze roamed over him. She
noted his commanding stance and bold stare. He
looked like a man who had done everything and
been everywhere.

His eyes narrowed as he gazed down at her. "You aren't going to tell me your name, are you?"

"No. I don't think I will."

"Any particular reason why not?"

"It's mine to give, and I don't think it's necessary to give it to you."

A mocking light glinted in his gray eyes. "It would have been more congenial if you had gone along with the proprieties, Joanna, but it doesn't matter in the long run."

Joanna stared at him. He, too, knew who she was! Did she wear a sign on her back, for Pete's sake? she wondered in irritation. The man whose foot she had stepped on had also known who she was. It was too much of a coincidence that two American men just happened to appear in the small English town where she was staying and knew her name.

Her hand clenched her catalogue. "I hope you enjoyed your little game, Mr. Tanner," she said tightly. "Do you usually ask questions you already know the answers to?"

"Do you usually go around bashing men's feet when they try to talk to you?"

"It's a habit I've only recently acquired. You might want to keep that in mind."

"I suppose I should be glad you haven't taken a dislike to one of my shoes too."

"Oh, I wouldn't tromp on your foot, Mr. Tanner. It's best to tread lightly around a man who wears a gun in the small of his back." Stepping around him, she said, "If you'll excuse me, Mr. Tanner. I have other paintings I want to see."

Stunned, Alex almost reached back to check for a

gun, but he caught himself. He hadn't worn a gun for over two years. What shocked him was that somehow Joanna Kerr had known he had worn one. He watched her walk away. She had won the first round.

Richard appeared beside him. "Things are running smoothly, I see."

"Shut up, Richard."

"Whatever you say, sir. I am only here to provide information, after all. The actual work is up to you." His gaze followed Joanna Kerr. "I hesitate to call getting acquainted with her work, however, but call me old-fashioned."

"You're old-fashioned," Alex said obligingly.

Moving away from the English agent, Alex waded through the crowd of people, his gaze on the woman across the room. His tactics were going to have to be revised. Getting the information he needed wasn't going to be as easy as he had originally thought.

Joanna felt the sharp edges of paper cutting into her palm and loosened her grip on the catalogue. She took a deep breath and forced herself to relax. She had come to the art exhibit as a favor to her grandmother, but it had been a big mistake. First, a man who introduced himself as Steven Canfield had made that ridiculous proposition, using her name as though he knew her, taking it for granted she would be thrilled to have dinner with him. Then when she turned down his invitation, he made the astonishing comment that her brother had said she would cooperate and invited her to his hotel room in London.

Her violent reaction had been as startling to him

as it had been to her. She'd regretted stomping on him as soon as she had done it, though not because she had assaulted his foot and his pride. He had deserved both injuries. By creating a scene, however, she had drawn attention to herself, and that was the last thing she wanted or needed. Her one consolation was that once the incident got back to her grandmother, the venerable old lady would only be amused, not horrified or embarrassed.

She stopped in front of a painting of a pastoral scene and wasn't at all surprised when a minute later Alex Tanner was standing beside her again. In a way she had been expecting him. She didn't think he was the type of man who gave up easily. If he had been sent by her father, she would quickly send him back but first she would let him play out his hand before she told him to cash in his chips.

"Put your arm around my waist," he said in a low voice.

She jerked her head around and stared at him in shock. "I beg your pardon?"

"Do it. You'll find out you were wrong about me."

She began to move away. "I'll take your word for it, Mr. Tanner."

He moved in front of her. Gripping her wrist, he guided her hand under his jacket to the back of his waist. His fingers spread out over hers to press them against his spine. She felt a leather belt but that was all.

No, she reconsidered. That wasn't all. Corded muscles and warm flesh were under the shirt. Her fingers stroked him for several seconds until she realized what she was doing.

Unsettled by her extreme reaction to him, she tugged her hand free. "You've made your point, Mr. Tanner. You don't wear a gun now, but you have in the past."

"What makes you think that?"

She noticed he didn't deny her statement. "If you know my name, you know who I am. Men like you have guarded my father ever since he's been in politics."

"Men like me?"

"You know what I mean. It's the way you stand, as though you're a coiled spring. It's in your eyes, like a hawk always on the watch for prey." She tilted her head to one side. "Would you like me to go on?"

"I get the picture."

She turned to leave, but his arm slid around her waist, stopping her. He securely anchored her to his side. "Not so fast. We still have a few things to discuss."

"No, we don't." Her heart was thudding too loudly, reacting to the heat emanating from his hard body. His hand was clamped around her waist, his thumb near her breast. She was vividly aware of a strong attraction, a current of electricity that pulsed around them.

Alex could feel her resistance to him, but he was also achingly aware of her slender body. He fought the temptation to move his thumb up a few tantalizing inches.

"All you have to do is relax," he said.

"All you have to do is say good-bye."

"I haven't and I won't."

"Look, Tanner, I neither want nor need a bodyguard."

"I'm glad to hear it. I'm not your bodyguard."

"Really?" Her voice held a touch of irony. "Exactly what are you then?"

"I'm a gardener."

She made a strangled sound of disbelief and amusement. "Of course you are."

With his free hand, he reached into the inside pocket of his leather jacket, withdrew a business card, and handed it to her. Glancing at it, Joanna saw the name TANNER LANDSCAPING INC., a telephone number and address in Houston, Texas, and his name printed in a lower corner. Alex Tanner, not Alexander, she noticed. The card could be real, she thought, but anyone could have a business card printed with whatever they wanted on it.

She started to hand it back. "Keep it," he said.

She shook her head. "I won't be needing it. I live in an apartment in Seattle, Mr. Tanner, which is a considerable distance from Houston the last time I looked at a map. I have two houseplants that I manage to water occasionally, but not one single blade of grass or a tree. I doubt if I'll have any need for your services." She tucked his card into the breast pocket of his jacket. "If you weren't sent by my father, then how did you know my name?"

"Your picture was in the local newspapers along with his when he was elected." He didn't add that he had first seen the newspaper clipping last week in Senator Kerr's office.

Joanna accepted his explanation since it could be true. What she found a bit hard to believe was that he remembered her from a black and white photo taken three years ago. Her father, with his mane of thick white hair and barrel-chested figure, was distinctive, but she had long accepted that her own appearance was ordinary and entirely forgettable. She didn't know why Alex Tanner was pretending to be interested in her, but she had enough on her mind without taking on any further problems.

"Well, Mr. Green Thumb, it's been fascinating, but I can only take so much excitement in one day." His grip had loosened enough for her to slip free. Keeping her expression as blank as possible, she met his gaze and said flatly, "Good-bye."

Joanna wound her way through the crowd, collected her tan cloth raincoat, then pushed open the door and stepped outside. It hadn't been much of a day weatherwise when she had left her grandmother's house at two o'clock, and now at four the overcast sky had decided to do something other than hover in a dull gray canopy. As it started to rain, she remembered her grandmother's warning to take an umbrella with her, a warning she unfortunately hadn't heeded. March in England was not known for providing many sunny days, and an umbrella was a sensible thing to have on hand.

If she had had any sense, she thought, she would have stayed home in the first place. This was not turning out to be one of her better days.

She started down the concrete steps outside the entrance and saw Steven Canfield standing at the bottom, looking up expectantly at her. She groaned inwardly. This definitely wasn't her day. She'd managed to get rid of one persistent man and was about to run smack into another.

Continuing down the steps, she said wearily, "Mr.

Canfield, I'm really not in the mood to hear any more of your colorful suggestions."

Canfield lifted his hand in a placating gesture. "I only wish to apologize. I was quite out of line. I would like to make it up to you by taking you out to dinner this evening, Miss Kerr."

The rain was coming down harder, and Joanna only wanted to get back to her grandmother's warm, dry, uncomplicated manor house. "I accept the apology, but I must refuse the dinner invitation. Now if you'll excuse me, I would like to get home and out of the rain."

He stepped in front of her as she tried to move around him, blocking her path as she reached the bottom step. "Then I'll drive you home. I think we should get better acquainted."

"No, thank you." How did he know she had walked? she wondered vaguely.

She again attempted to get around him, but he stopped her by taking hold of her upper arm. His voice was no longer pleasant but slightly threatening. "I insist."

Before she could break his hold, a masculine voice behind her said menacingly, "Drop your hand or look forward to seeing it in a cast."

Canfield's eyes widened as his gaze shifted from Joanna to the tall man standing behind her who had appeared unexpectedly. He dropped his hand away from Joanna and blustered, "I was just going to drive Miss Kerr home."

"She doesn't appear to want to go with you."

The rain was coming down steadily, and Joanna was becoming increasingly wet and uncomfortable.

Leaving the two men to settle their differences on their own, she began to walk away. A firm hand at her waist changed her direction toward the car park.

Resisting his grip on her, she whirled around. "I don't want to go with you either, Mr. Tanner."

"I guess I was wrong about you," he said calmly, not breaking his stride and bringing her easily along with him. "I thought you had enough sense to get in out of the rain."

He stopped on the left side, the passenger side, of a silver-gray Jaguar and unlocked the door. Opening it, he gestured for her to get in. When she made no move to do so, he said silkily, "We can do this the easy way or the hard way, but either way, I'm driving you home."

Whether it was the threat implied in his voice or her curiosity, Joanna slid onto the leather seat, arranging her damp skirt around her legs. He joined her in the car and started the engine. He turned the dial of the heater, and warm air began to circulate. The collar of his jacket had been pulled up around his neck, and he folded it back in place. Then he turned to look at her.

Joanna was aware that through her open coat the rain had dampened her knit dress. It clung to her, leaving little of her shape to the imagination. Since there was nothing she could do about it, she decided to ignore it, hoping he would do the same. It was a vain hope. She could feel his gaze on her breasts as though he were stroking them.

She lifted her chin and faced him. "Are you unfamiliar with a right-hand drive car, Mr. Tanner?"

He saw the challenge in her eyes and a corner of

his mouth curled in a slow smile. "Are you afraid I'll drive you into a ditch?"

"I was wondering if you could figure out where first gear is."

He didn't take the less than subtle hint. "I would rather talk to you without having to divide my attention between you and the road."

She crossed her arms in front of her, hoping she looked more relaxed than she felt. "I could have handled Canfield without your help. I doubt if I'll have any more run-ins with obnoxious men during my stay here."

Her expression clearly included him under the heading of obnoxious men. A faint rhythmic sound drew his gaze to the floor on her side of the car. Her foot was tapping the rubber mat. His smile broadened. It seemed Miss Joanna Kerr had a temper. He didn't waste time debating whether or not she could have gotten rid of the other man since he had already done it for her.

"What did that guy say to you earlier to make you angry enough to stomp on his foot?" he asked casually.

She bluntly repeated Canfield's proposition, adding, "He seemed to think dropping my brother's name would cinch it."

Alex fought down sudden fury at hearing what the other man had said to her, but he managed to retain a blank expression. "It didn't seem to work. Is your brother in England too?"

She didn't know what that had to do with anything, but she answered him anyway. "I don't know. I doubt it, but with Travis, it's hard to predict where he's at or what he's doing."

Alex knew Travis had been in D.C. a little more than a week ago but he wasn't there now. "Apparently he knew where you were. He told Canfield you were here."

She looked skeptical. "Or Canfield has other reasons for being here."

"Such as?"

"He could work for you."

"Why do you think I know him?"

"Canfield's an American, and he knew my name. You did, too, and it's unusual for Americans to be coming out of the woodwork all of a sudden in Chesham. This isn't exactly a booming tourist town."

Alex filed the name Canfield in his mind to be checked on later. She was right. It was too much of a coincidence. "I've never seen him before today."

She shrugged, either meaning she didn't believe him or didn't particularly care. "I still don't need a bodyguard, Mr. Tanner. I'll accept a ride home since you didn't give me much choice. But after you drop me off, you can go back to my father and tell him I refused to let you follow me around. That will get you off the hook."

"I told you, I'm not your bodyguard."

"Why are you in Chesham then, Mr. Tanner? Chesham used to be known for its lace-making and straw-plaiting industries, and there's a brush factory here now, but the closest nursery of any size is in Beaconsfield, about ten miles away."

He was ready with a prepared excuse. "There are several well-known orchid growers in England I buy cuttings from and have them sent back to Houston."

"There were no orchid cuttings at the art exhibit."

"I saw a notice about the art exhibit posted in the window at a newsagents, and I thought it would be something to do on a Saturday afternoon." He paused, then added, "It turned out to be more interesting than I thought."

Joanna knew everything he said could be legitimate, yet somehow it didn't fit. Her father had been in public life for a long time. She was familiar with the kind of men who had protected him ever since he moved to the capital, and especially since he had been involved in several controversial criminal investigations. He had made enemies, and as a result, security measures had been taken. Those measures included bodyguards, well-trained men and women who were experts in guarding people or possessions, and who were comfortable with guns and surveillance. She glanced at the man in the car with her. Alex Tanner had the same alert, waiting quality she had seen in the people who protected her father. He might be the owner of a landscaping company now, but he hadn't always been involved in things as innocent and as nonthreatening as plants.

She shook her head. "I don't buy it," she murmured.

Alex had the feeling she wouldn't. "Buy what?"

"This whole thing. Two American men pop up in a small town on the same day and both just happen to know who I am. All of a sudden, I have two men fighting for my company. That should be flattering, but it's a little hard to swallow since it's not a problem I've ever had before. I didn't just fall off the turnip truck, Tanner. Something's going on, and I'd like to know what it is since I seem to be involved in it."

Alex stared out the windshield while he thought

about what she had said. When the senator had asked him to go to England to enlist Joanna's cooperation one way or the other, Alex had thought it would take only a couple of days. But that was before he met her. She wasn't going to be as easy to charm or to fool as he originally thought.

Coming to a decision, he shifted into first gear. The senator had insisted Joanna wasn't involved in Travis's latest escapade. Alex hadn't automatically accepted Franklyn's opinion. After meeting Joanna, however, he decided to trust her. Later, if he was proved wrong, he would deal with it.

Joanna's mouth twisted ruefully as she watched him. He wasn't going to tell her anything. She was disappointed but not really surprised. At least it looked as if he was finally going to drive her home.

As he left the community center's car park, she said, "I'm staying with my grandmother who lives at the top of the hill on Chartridge Lane. If you turn left . . ." She saw he was already turning left before she had finished giving him the directions. "I see you already know where my grandmother lives."

He shook his head, keeping his attention on the narrow street. "Every time I've asked for directions in England, everyone starts from High Street. I don't imagine Chesham is any different."

She shook her head. "Turn right at the War Memorial in the middle of town. At the top of the hill, there's an open gate in the middle of a stone wall."

She thought she had given fairly clear instructions, but he drove past the solitary figure of the War Memorial without taking the turnoff for Chartridge Lane.

"All right, Tanner," she said tightly. "I think I've been fairly good-natured up to this point, but kidnapping is going a bit far, even for you."

"I'm not kidnapping you. I want to talk to you, and I doubt if you want your grandmother to hear what we're going to discuss." His gaze flicked to the rearview mirror. "Besides, your persistent admirer is following us."

"Who?"

"Canfield."

He stopped the car to allow a young woman pushing a pram to cross the street, and used the opportunity to look at Joanna. She was watching the woman maneuver the large wheels of the pram over the curb. He had expected Joanna to look back to verify what he had said, but she didn't.

He hadn't driven very far when she ordered, "Turn right."

He turned onto a narrow street, noting that the small tan Cortina paused briefly before following them, keeping a discreet distance between them. Alex kept driving until Joanna said, "Pull into that small driveway next to the antique shop. You can park alongside the building on the left."

There was only room for one car in the space she indicated, so Canfield would have to either keep going or block the street if he parked at the curb. Joanna couldn't have chosen a better spot. He wondered if she was aware of that.

Turning off the engine, he looked over at her, but she was opening her door. There wasn't much room between the car and the wall of the building, but she managed to squeeze through the small opening.

As Alex got out of the car, he saw the Cortina slowly drive by and could tell the moment Canfield spotted him and the car. Canfield sped up and continued on.

Joanna was walking toward the street without looking back to see if Alex was following her. His long stride caught him up with her as she was stepping off the curb, and he walked beside her as they crossed the street. They passed over a small wooden bridge that spanned a trickling stream. Alex rarely allowed anyone else to take control of a situation, but his curiosity kept him silent at her side, waiting to see where she was headed.

She glanced up the road and saw Canfield pull into a driveway and then back up, apparently planning to come back in their direction. Taking Alex's arm, she dashed around a corner and quickly pulled him through a doorway. On the small sign hanging over the entrance was a faded painting of a woman wearing a crown and, in gothic script, "The Queen's Head."

Inside, Joanna let go of his arm and went up to the wooden bar. She ordered a half-pint of lager for herself and a pint of the same for Alex without bothering to ask him his preference. She paid for the drinks when the glass mugs were placed on the bar, then carried them over to a table near a stone fireplace where several fat logs were burning slowly.

A pair of elderly men were playing a game of dominoes at another table, their concentration solely on the tiles. A solitary woman sipping a delicate glass of sherry sat in a corner, a dog of questionable breeding lay on the floor at her feet.

Alex pulled out the chair that faced the door and sat down as Joanna removed her damp coat and laid it over the back of the chair next to her. Her drink remained untouched as she leaned back and calmly met his gaze.

"Very nicely done," he said quietly, lifting his pint in a salute. "It makes me wonder if you've had to do this type of thing before."

"Believe it or not, this is the first time." Her voice had a chilly edge. "I didn't want to be interrupted by Mr. Canfield while you're telling me what in hell is going on. Would I be correct in assuming all this has something to do with my brother Travis?"

Stalling, Alex asked, "All what?"

Counting off on her fingers, she listed, "You, the sweet-talking Mr. Canfield, your simultaneous appearance in England at a small, local art exhibit, Canfield dropping Travis's name, you asking if Travis is in England, Canfield following us."

Alex took a swallow of lager and set the pint down. "You want the truth?"

"It would be a nice change."

He ignored her sarcasm. "Your brother is going to be getting in touch with you soon, and it's important that you tell me when he does."

As an explanation, Joanna thought, that left gaps the size of the Grand Canyon. "I see." Leaning her elbow on the table, she cupped her chin in her palm and asked conversationally, "And why would he be contacting me, and why do you have to know about it if he does?"

Alex found himself captivated by the golden lights in her dark brown eyes. His priorities were shifting with each passing minute he was with her. She was becoming much more interesting than the reason for his visit to England.

He forced his attention back to her questions. "Your brother has taken something that doesn't belong to him. It belongs to the government, and they want it back. In the note your brother sent to your father, he stated you will be used as a mediator between them. Travis apparently didn't know you had gone to England at the time he wrote the note, but he must know you're here now if Canfield is his messenger boy. When Travis contacts you, I need you to find out where he is and then tell me."

Joanna sat up straight. It sounded like Travis had gotten himself into deep trouble this time. "What did Travis steal?"

Alex's expression didn't change, but his eyes lost their amused glimmer. "It's not necessary for you to know the details."

"But it's necessary for me to turn my brother over to you."

"You only have to tell me where he is. I'll do the rest."

Joanna studied him closely. She wouldn't want to be Travis when this man eventually found him. And Alex Tanner would find him, with or without her help.

She knew she didn't stand a chance in hell of getting a straight answer, but she tried anyway. "Why did my father ask you to come all this way to talk to me?"

"He knows I'll do the job the way he wants it done."

"So all that stuff about orchid cuttings and Tanner Landscaping was part of a line to charm me out of some information?"

He shook his head. "There really is a Tanner Landscaping, and I really am a gardener."

"But you weren't always a gardener."

He continued to look at her, but he didn't reply. Instead he picked up his pint and drank.

She sighed with resignation. "I didn't really expect an answer." Leaning back, she crossed her arms in front of her. "So how do I get in touch with you if I hear from Travis?"

Smiling slowly, Alex took his time answering. "You won't have to. I plan on being with you."

Two

Joanna stared at him in openmouthed astonishment. "You plan on being with me where?"

"Wherever you are."

She had ordered her lager only as a prop, an excuse to be in the pub. Now she took a healthy swallow of the warm beer, aware that Alex was watching her, that faint smile still curving his mouth.

She set her mug back down, cleared her throat, and said fatalistically, "All right, I'll bite. How do you plan to work this being with me wherever I am?"

"It's very simple. Whatever you plan to do, I'll do it with you."

He wasn't making a threat or even a promise, she thought. It was a quiet statement of fact. Still, she couldn't resist a little jab. "I bet your plants grow real well in Texas, Mr. Tanner. You certainly can spread a fine field of . . . fertilizer."

His rich, masculine laughter sent shivers up her

spine as it filled their corner of the room, blending with the crackling fire and the clatter of the domino tiles.

Still smiling, Alex pushed back his chair and stood up. "I'll take you home," he said, holding Joanna's coat for her, "and you can introduce me to your grandmother. She might as well get used to seeing me around."

She should stop this nonsense now, Joanna told herself. All she had to do was tell him she didn't want to be involved. She didn't have to cooperate with him to find Travis or help him get back whatever Travis had stolen. There were plenty of professionals experienced in finding people who broke the law, if that's what Travis had done. She wouldn't be surprised if Alex Tanner was one of those professionals, even though he insisted he was in the landscaping business. So why didn't he get on with his search, she wondered for about the third time, and leave her out of it?

She had a few problems of her own to straighten out, and she didn't need any more at the moment. Besides, Travis hadn't contacted her. There was a chance he wouldn't, so Alex Tanner could be wasting his time and hers.

He was still holding her coat for her, so she turned her back to him and slid her arms into the sleeves. Briefly, she felt his hands resting on her shoulders as she adjusted the collar, his fingers firm and strong. It was a strangely intimate gesture for such a simple act.

Slowly, she revolved to face him, her gaze sweeping up to meet his smoky gray eyes. He gazed seriously at her for a long moment. The sound of a chair scraping across the wooden floor broke the spell around them. Joanna tied her belt tightly around her waist and took a deep, steadying breath.

"We'd better go see if our shadow is lurking outside."

Alex nodded and took her arm. There was no sign of a tan Cortina when they left the pub and returned to Alex's car. It wasn't necessary for Joanna to repeat the directions to her grandmother's house. This time Alex took the turnoff he was supposed to have taken before and drove up Chartridge Lane.

The stone wall appeared on their right and Alex steered the car easily through the open gates. A narrow lane wound between trees and hedges, and the tires crunched on the loose gravel. A stately red brick manor house with leaded windows and a recessed entrance came into view as they rounded a gentle curve. A green lawn stretched out in front of the house, big enough to hold a tennis court with room left over. Tall trees and plump shrubbery blocked any view of the stone wall surrounding the grounds.

Alex parked in front of the house and reached to turn off the ignition, but Joanna's hand stopped him. "This is as far as we go, Mr. Tanner." She dropped her hand and added, "Thanks for driving me home."

As she turned and reached for the doorlatch, she felt his hand on her arm, his grip strong enough to prevent her from getting out of the car. She looked at him over her shoulder. For a minute the only sounds were the wipers slashing across the windshield and the heater fan continuing to blow warm air.

"Invite me in," he said softly.

She turned in the seat to face him squarely. "Look, Tanner. This has gone far enough. I'm not going to have my grandmother upset by hearing Travis is in trouble again. Whatever he's done has nothing to do with her."

"Apparently I haven't made it clear that Travis is in serious trouble, Joanna. It's important to get this resolved quickly and with a minimum of fuss. I'll do whatever I have to to accomplish that."

She could feel the heat of his hand through her coat sleeve, sparking a strange stirring deep inside her. Finally she said, "If he does call me or come here, I'll let you know."

Since she had removed her hand from the latch and was making no move to leave the car, Alex released her arm. "How do you plan to do that? You don't know where I'm staying."

"You could tell me," she said with exaggerated patience. "Then I would know."

He would have preferred to stay with her longer, but he had the feeling if he insisted, he would lose what little ground he had gained. He took out the business card she had put back in his pocket and grabbed a pen off the dashboard, then wrote down the name of his hotel in Amersham, a small town three miles from Chesham. There were no hotels or inns in Chesham, and it had been the closest accommodations he could find. He didn't hold much hope she would call him, but he held the card out to her anyway.

Joanna took the card. For a moment, she looked at his handwriting without seeing the words written there. She knew he wouldn't stop her from getting out of the car this time, but now she was oddly reluctant to go. It didn't make sense. Slowly she raised her eyes to his. What was it about this man that called to her senses? she wondered with a hint of panic.

She had never felt this instant awareness around a man before. Her heart beat faster, and her skin felt sensitized as though the air were charged with electricity. She didn't understand it, but she knew it existed.

Without realizing it, she used his name for the first time. "Alex," she said abruptly, "you don't suspect me of being Travis's accomplice?"

Heat quivered through him at the sound of his name on her lips. "No," he said.

"That's it? A flat no?"

"Yes."

"Why?" She didn't know why it was important but it was. "Because my father told you I wasn't involved?"

"Senator Kerr insisted you had nothing to do with the theft." His gaze settled briefly on her mouth, then slid up to meet her expressive eyes. "I wasn't sure until I met you."

Joanna didn't know exactly how to take his last comment, but then her usual mental faculties weren't exactly charging on all cylinders. She slid his card into the pocket of her coat and looked away, her gaze going to one of the leaded windows. She saw a curtain move back into place, and she sighed heavily. "My grandmother knows someone has brought me home. You'll have to come in or I'll be subjected to a lecture on good manners." Suddenly, she smiled. "I hope you like tea."

Whether it was for the sake of their audience or because he simply beat her to the punch, Alex was out of the car and opening her door before she had a chance to open it herself. He extended his hand to her, and after a slight hesitation, she placed her hand in his and allowed him to help her from the car.

The housekeeper opened the front door for them. Stella Deerborn was a slim, gray-haired woman in her late sixties with a frank gaze behind small oval wire-framed glasses. She closely examined the man standing beside her employer's granddaughter, and was obviously displeased with what she saw.

Four dogs in a variety of sizes, shapes, and shades suddenly bounded outside from behind the housekeeper. Tails wagged and tongues licked in the dogs' eagerness to greet the two people about to enter their domain.

Joanna patted each head and noticed Alex automatically reaching down to scratch ears and stroke the furry head closest to him.

One of the larger dogs jumped up on her, his front paws landing on her belted waist. "Get down, Obie," she said. "You know better than that."

Alex gently pushed the large paws off Joanna. "Obie?"

"This is Obediah." Going on to the other dogs, she introduced them one by one. "Cricket, Winston, and Crumpet."

"Your grandmother obviously prefers more imaginative names than Rover and Spot."

"My grandmother has a habit of taking in strays that no one else wants, and she believes they should have distinctive names to make up for their lack of breeding."

"Your grandmother was becoming concerned about you, Miss Joanna," Stella said sternly.

Joanna was accustomed to Stella voicing her opinions by saying they were her employer's views and not her own.

Before she could reply, Alex took the blame for her tardiness. "It's my fault. I insisted on giving her a ride home since it was raining."

"That should have speeded her arrival, not delayed it." Begrudgingly, Stella opened the door wider and stepped aside. "Your grandmother is about to have tea."

"This is Alex Tanner, Stella. He'll be joining us for tea."

The older woman's reply was a gruff hrumph that could have meant anything. She waited for them to remove their coats, then disappeared through an arched doorway with their coats in her possession.

Alex stared after the formidable woman. "Is it me in particular or men in general she doesn't like?"

"That's just her way. When I was younger, she used to scare me silly until I realized her bark is worse than her bite. Under that gruff exterior is a kindhearted soul who is devoted to my grandmother." She began walking down the hall. "My grandmother will be in the drawing room."

Elizabeth Montain was seated in a regal Queen Anne chair reading a book. Dressed in a gray suit with a white silk blouse, Joanna's grandmother could easily pass for a woman twenty years younger than her actual age of seventy. A widow for over fifteen years, Elizabeth was softly elegant, exuding warmth and charm. Her dark hair displayed a generous sprinkling of gray and was casually arranged in a twist at the back of her head. She was composed and neat, but humor was evident in the lines radiating from the corners of her eyes and the soft curve of her mouth.

She extended her hand to Alex after Joanna made the introductions. "Welcome to Larksridge House, Mr. Tanner."

If Elizabeth was surprised Joanna had brought a man home with her, she gave no indication in either her voice or her expression. Alex wondered if Joanna made a habit of bringing men home to her grandmother, like one of the stray dogs. For some strange reason that thought didn't sit very well with him.

Joanna sat down on the sofa. Although there was an unoccupied chair, Alex ignored it and sat down on the sofa beside Joanna. She was conscious of his thigh only a few inches away from hers, and tried to suppress her awareness of him. She couldn't. It was amazingly difficult to make normal conversation when her whole being was centered on the man sitting beside her.

Pouring tea after Stella had set the tray down in front of her, Elizabeth told Joanna there had been a phone call for her. "It was a gentleman. He wouldn't leave his name, but he said it was important he talk to you. I told him you were attending the art exhibit at the Whitehill Community Centre." She smiled at Alex. "I see I did the right thing by telling you where she was."

Alex accepted the dainty cup and saucer she held out to him. Joanna's grandmother was taking it for granted he was the man who had called, and he didn't contradict her. He had known where Joanna was going to be because he had called her father early that morning. The senator had spoken to Elizabeth the previous day, and she had mentioned Joanna would be attending the art exhibit. The man who had phoned could have been either Canfield or Travis.

For the next hour, Elizabeth poured tea, passed around delicate slivers of cakes and biscuits, and asked Alex gently probing questions about his personal life.

After he told her he had been raised on a ranch but now lived in a suburb of Houston, she asked, "Why did you leave the ranch, Mr. Tanner?"

"I wanted to see a bit of the world. I wasn't ready to be tied down."

"Is that why you've never married? You wanted to taste freedom before having a family?"

Alex gave the older woman a half smile. "Perhaps."

Elizabeth asked about the places he had been, and he answered without telling her anything specific. Elizabeth may not have noticed the evasions, but Joanna did.

He soon guided the conversation to plants, easily throwing in terms like cattleya and cymbidium, as he explained he was in England to look at orchids. Elizabeth asked about the seedlings he was planning on buying. From the way he described his landscape business, Joanna got the impression it was more than a small local nursery catering to the needs of weekend gardening enthusiasts.

"How did you become involved in the landscape business, Mr. Tanner?" Elizabeth asked.

"I used to help my brother, Brian, with his botany experiments when he was home from college in the summers. I learned a great deal from him, and I discovered I liked working in the soil, making things grow."

"You're very young to have your own company. How long have you been in the business?"

Alex didn't consider thirty-six particularly young, but he didn't contradict her. "I've had the company a little over two years. I bought the business from my brother when he took a job teaching botany at a college in California."

He was like a chameleon, Joanna thought, watching him over the rim of her cup. He changed to suit his surroundings. The aggression he had shown toward her was tamped down now as he chatted with her grandmother as though he had known her for years.

He might be a gardener, but there was a quiet authority, a self-confidence about him that had been formed in his past. She didn't believe he had become the man he was by simply working the soil. She had the feeling he had been forged and hardened by unusual challenges and confrontations.

When he eventually stood up to leave, she wasn't at all surprised when her grandmother invited him to come again. And she had no doubt he would take advantage of that offer in the near future. He had come to England on a mission, and she didn't think he was a man who would give up until he had completed what he had set out to do.

She escorted him to the door, and he paused on the threshold. "I like your grandmother."

"It seems to be mutual."

He smiled. "I'll see you tomorrow."

"Will you?"

Lifting his hand, he touched the knuckle of his forefinger to her cheek, an intimate gesture that surprised them both. "You can count on it." He dropped his hand and his voice changed, losing its warmth and becoming cool and businesslike. "If Travis calls tonight, you can reach me at the Crown Hotel in Amersham. It doesn't matter what time it is, let me know."

She nodded but didn't make any comment. With one last unfathomable look, Alex left.

The following morning with Stella's grocery list in one hand and a wicker shopping basket in the other, Joanna strolled along the aisles of Waitroses, choosing the items Stella wanted. There were only a few things to buy in the grocery store before she went on to the bakery and the butcher shop. She studied the last item on her list and frowned. Over the years she had become accustomed to the different names the British used, but this one had her stumped. Three swedes. She smiled. It would be interesting to see Stella's reaction if she brought home three Swedish men.

The back of her neck suddenly prickled with awareness, and she turned her head to see Alex reading her list over her shoulder. He was dressed casually in jeans, a blue shirt, and a dark blue jacket with epaulets on each shoulder, and her breath caught in her throat at the sight of him. He had a quality of confidence that draped him like a cloak, and she found herself intrigued by him more and more.

"Don't tell me you just happen to be doing your grocery shopping," she said.

"I am now. Stella told me where you were." He smiled. "After only one grumble and two scowls."

"Travis hasn't called."

"I know."

His complacent tone irritated her. "What do you mean, you know?"

"You didn't come to the hotel or call. You would have done one or the other if Travis had contacted you."

"You think you know me so well, Mr. Tanner?"

"I was Alex yesterday."

She drew her attention back to the list. "I have a problem."

"You certainly do if you keep calling me Mr. Tanner."

Giving him a rather pained smile, she held out the list. "Look at this. Three swedes. I know that in England chips are french fries, crisps are potato chips, an aubergine is an eggplant, but I'm stumped by swede. I don't know if it's vegetable, animal, or mineral. I'll have to ask one of the clerks."

Alex stayed with her as a clerk helped her choose three yellow turnips, then Alex accompanied her through the checkout line. She told him customers bagged their own groceries, and he obligingly put her purchases back in her wicker basket. Being a bag boy wasn't what he'd had in mind when he came looking for her, he thought, but it was better than not being with her at all.

She had remained in his mind after he had left her last night, a constant presence niggling at him even in his sleep. That had never happened to him before, and it was disconcerting enough to try to figure out why. In order to do that, he had to spend some time with her, even if it meant bagging groceries. The hard part was remembering he had another reason for being with her.

She tucked her change into her purse and indicated the laden basket. "Since you obviously plan to come with me, you can carry the groceries."

Her imperious tone made him smile. Murmuring, "Yes, Ma'am," with mock meekness, he picked up the basket and followed her out of the grocery store. The basket got a little heavier with each stop she made. From the grocery store she went to the bakery for a loaf of freshly baked bread, then to Brazil's Butcher Shop, where she ordered rashers of bacon and minced beef, which looked remarkably like hamburger.

Outside the greengrocer she chose a tied bundle of fresh flowers from a tin bucket. "I'll carry these."

"You're enjoying this, aren't you? Turning me into your glorified box boy is your subtle way of getting a little of your own back."

She buried her nose briefly in the fragrant blossoms and then lowered the flowers. "Yes, I am enjoying this. Aren't you?"

Strangely enough he was, he realized. "I've done many things with a beautiful woman, but this is the first time I've been a bearer to one."

Joanna wasn't going to ask what he usually did with women. She had a good idea and it had nothing to do with shopping.

"I'm through with the shopping," she said. "Are you planning on coming back to my grandmother's with me?"

"Are you asking me?"

Her gaze never faltered as she met his. "Would it make any difference if I did?"

"Probably not, but it would be a nice surprise."

She couldn't help wondering if they were talking about the same thing. "I wouldn't want it said I got in the way of you doing your job. I walked, so unless you have your car downtown, you will have to trudge up the hill with me."

Shifting the basket to his other hand, he slipped his arm through hers and began to walk in the direction of Chartridge Lane. "I left my car at your grandmother's. And," he added, sounding extremely satisfied with himself, "I've been invited to lunch."

"You are one of the most arrogant men I've ever met. No. Let me rephrase that. You *are* the most arrogant man I've ever met. A steamroller is a Tinkertoy compared to you."

He grinned down at her. "I like you too."

She choked and nearly tripped over her own feet, but his arm kept her from falling. The man should be put away somewhere, she decided, preferably in a room with padded walls and strong locks. While they walked up the hill, she considered several alternate places she would like Alex Tanner to go, all of them far, far away and extremely uncomfortable.

The problem was, she kept picturing herself locked in that room with him.

Her grandmother welcomed Alex with a warm smile and ushered him through the house to the back garden to show him her prize roses. Feeling oddly abandoned, Joanna went into the kitchen with the full shopping basket. She set it on the wooden table with a loud thump.

The housekeeper raised an eyebrow as she noted

Joanna's annoyed expression. "You look as cross as two sticks, Miss Joanna. Usually you come back from the shops laughing about some remark someone made. Am I correct in assuming you found nothing humorous in the shops this morning?"

"You are correct. And I also don't find anything amusing about the tall Texan I brought back with me. He said he has been invited to lunch."

Stella made one of her notable sounds of displeasure. For such a respectable looking woman, she could come up with some rather undignified responses. "So your grandmother informed me earlier. I'm to pull out all the stops to fix him a substantial lunch, she says, as excited as I've ever seen her except when she knows you're coming to visit."

Joanna began putting away the things she had purchased. "If having Alex Tanner come to lunch makes her happy, we'll have to go along with it. I've upset her enough. I won't make a fuss about him, because she seems to enjoy his company."

"You haven't upset her, Miss Joanna," Stella said. "Your grandmother understands you have a right to know the true circumstances of your birth. It's just that it's not pleasant for her to dredge it all up again after so many years."

"I know it was selfish of me to burden her with what Travis told me. I didn't want to believe him when he told me Franklyn Kerr wasn't really my father. Even when I confronted Dad with Travis's story and he confirmed it, I still couldn't bring myself to accept it. Maybe I was secretly hoping Grandmother would say it was all a lie. For twenty-five years, I've been the daughter of Franklyn Kerr, and suddenly I'm not. It takes a little getting used to."

"I imagine it does, but if anyone can adjust, it's you, Miss Joanna. You've always been a strong girl."

"I don't feel very strong at the moment. I want to understand what happened. That's all."

Stella filled the electric teakettle with cold water and flicked the switch on. "Your mother was very young and innocent when she met Stuart, Franklyn's brother. It wasn't her fault he was killed in that climbing accident before they could be married. At first, Miss Amelia was quite distraught when she knew you were on the way. You know how proper your grandmother is. To have her daughter with child out of wedlock was shameful to her. Franklyn did the right thing by marrying your mother and giving her child the Kerr name, which was rightfully yours."

Joanna watched Stella measure tea into a plump brown teapot. Since she arrived three days ago, the teapot had been constantly in use, for it was Stella's remedy for difficult situations. She took down two cups and saucers and set them on the small table in front of the wide window. Stella was certainly going to need her cup of tea, Joanna mused, when she told her more bad news.

After Stella had poured their tea, Joanna said, "Travis is in trouble again."

"That doesn't surprise me. That boy seems to attract it. What is it this time?"

Joanna recited the little bit Alex had told her. "The only reason Alex Tanner is here is to find out where Travis is and get back whatever he stole. I made him promise not to say anything about Travis's latest problem to Grandmother. She thinks Alex is here because he's interested in me, and I'm going to let her continue to think that."

Stella's sharp eyes drilled into Joanna with all the perception of her years. "I can understand why she believes he's interested in you. His eyes follow you whenever you're near him."

Joanna would have liked to deny Stella's claim, but she had seen Alex watching her too.

Stella's spoon clanked against the sides of her china cup as she stirred her tea. "One can only hope you don't start looking back at him the same way. We don't need any of that boy-girl foolishness around here."

Joanna silently agreed, a smile tugging at her lips at the housekeeper's phrase. She didn't need any of that boy-girl foolishness either. Actually, it was the last thing she needed, especially if Alex was the boy. She quickly amended that thought and her smile faded. Alex Tanner was no boy. He was a grown man who had the instincts of a hunter and a latent sensuality that drew a response from her as naturally as breathing.

The clink of Stella's cup being placed on its saucer brought Joanna's attention back to the housekeeper. Stella was looking out the window to the back garden. Following the other woman's gaze, Joanna saw her grandmother and Alex slowly strolling back to the house. Elizabeth's arm was laced through his.

Steeling herself like an actor about to go onstage, Joanna stood up and rinsed out her cup in the sink. Act Two was about to begin.

While they ate lunch, Elizabeth was successful in uncovering more about Alex's background. Joanna was surprised when he said he was the youngest of nine children. His eight brothers had been his examples, his teachers, and his companions on their remote Texas ranch. His mother had died shortly after he had been born, and he had been raised in an all-male environment. When he was eight, his father died after falling off a barn roof he had been repairing. Alex's oldest brother, Eric, had become the head of the household.

"Eric is six foot seven in his boots, so his size alone kept us in line. Later, we all grew to respect him. He was our father, our brother, and as strange as it sounds, our mother too."

"He sounds like an exceptional man," Elizabeth said gently.

Alex told them about the first time he had ridden a horse alone, when he was four. It turned out to be the first time he fell off a horse too. Before then, he had ridden with one of his brothers, but Eric had decided it was time for him to ride solo. His brothers tossed him back up on the horse each time he fell off, until he finally managed to stay on.

"I should have realized what I was in for when Eric told me the horse's name was Buckaroo," Alex said dryly. "I quickly learned why when he kept bucking me off."

Elizabeth looked faintly shocked. "Couldn't your brother have chosen a more gentle horse or a pony for you to ride?"

Alex shook his head. "Eric taught me a valuable lesson. If something is too easy, there's no satisfaction in conquering it. Anything that comes easy isn't worth having." His gaze shifted to Joanna. "I've found that applies to a number of situations."

Joanna raised her brows. "They also must have taught you, it pays to have a hard head or rear end, depending on what hits the ground first."

Her grandmother gave her a disapproving look. A man's lower anatomy didn't fall into the category of subjects one used in polite conversation. Changing the subject abruptly, Elizabeth said, "Joanna, I have wonderful news. Alex has generously offered to help put the apple orchard in shape when he can spare the time from his business appointments. There are a number of trees that need to be replaced, and I would like you to show him where the nurseries are so he can pick out new trees."

Joanna caught a flicker of amusement in his eyes as she turned back to her grandmother. "Of course. I would be happy to tell Mr. Tanner where he can go."

Elizabeth missed the insinuation in her reply, but Alex didn't. His lips curved upward, and Joanna knew he was thoroughly enjoying himself . . . at her expense.

Her grandmother smiled brightly. "Splendid. I knew I could count on you. But perhaps it would be better if you accompanied him to the nurseries personally." As an afterthought, she added, "Oh, I almost forgot. I've invited Alex to be our houseguest during the remaining time he is in England. I would like you to go with him to collect his things at the hotel in Amersham. It's the least we can do, since he will be giving us the benefit of his landscaping skills."

Joanna's mouth dropped open in astonishment. For her grandmother to invite a virtual stranger to stay under her roof was unbelievable. Elizabeth still considered the man next door a relative newcomer, and he had lived in the neighborhood for twenty years. Her grandmother might take in stray dogs, but this was the first time she had invited a man she had just met to be a houseguest.

Joanna jerked her head around and her angry gaze slammed into Alex's. He calmly lifted his cup of coffee in a mock salute, his eyes holding hers in a challenge as old as time.

Three

When they reached his room at the Crown Hotel, Alex shut the door behind them and leaned against it, his arms crossed over his chest. "Okay, let me have it."

The room was small with only enough space for a single bed, a dresser, and a wardrobe. Standing between the bed and the dresser, Joanna turned to face him. "Let you have what?"

"Did you know you tap your toes when you're angry?"

That was only one of a number of other things he'd noticed about her, he thought. He could also have told her how her flashing eyes and proud stance aroused him when she was angry, and how badly he wanted to touch her. Why should now be any different? he asked himself ruefully. All she had to do was enter a room and his body would harden. Everything about her sent waves of molten heat rushing through his veins. When she was angry, his guts tied in knots at the thought of her fury changing into passion. When she smiled, it was worse.

Joanna glanced down at her foot and saw he was right. "So I am." Damn his sharp eyes, she thought. He noticed too darn much. "If I spend any more time with you, I'll wear out my shoes."

"We're alone now. Your grandmother can't hear your shocking language when you blast away at me. So go ahead. I can take it."

There were so many accusations she wanted to make, she didn't know where to begin. She just chose the first one that came to her. "Was it really necessary for you to get yourself invited to stay at my grandmother's home? I told you I would let you know if Travis contacted me. Last night I made a few phone calls in an attempt to find him, but no one seems to have seen him. I would have told you if I had learned anything. But you want to stay at my grandmother's and keep an eye on me. You don't really trust me, do you?"

"Perhaps I'm trying to make it easier for you," he said quietly.

She shook her head. "No, I think it's because you don't trust me. If you did, you would tell me what Travis has stolen. All you've said is that he's taken something and my father sent you here to be on hand when Travis contacts me. You don't have to live in my back pocket to make sure you're there when and if Travis gets in touch with me."

"I can think of worse places to be," he drawled, his gaze running over her slim hips covered by dark brown linen slacks.

She ignored his provocative statement, although

she had to drag her mind away from the thought of his hands sliding over her hips.

Forcing badly needed breath into her lungs, she cleared her throat and forced her attention back to the point she was trying to make. "Do you know the real reason my grandmother invited you to stay at the house?"

He nodded. "The sadly neglected apple orchard and her penchant for taking in strays. I'll get your grandmother's trees in shape and have the added advantage of being there when Travis calls you. I would say everyone benefits all the way around."

She wished he wouldn't keep looking at her so intently. 'You aren't as clever as you think. You just walked into my grandmother's matchmaking trap. She's trying to throw us together in the hope we'll become involved."

He pushed away from the door and in two long strides was standing in front of her. He allowed only his gaze to touch her as he looked down at her. "What your grandmother doesn't realize is we're already involved. We have been from the moment I first touched you."

"Oh, no." She raised her hand as though to ward him off and took a step back. "The only thing between us is this situation with Travis. Once he contacts me and I tell you what he said, you'll go chase him down. That's the extent of our involvement."

"Hmm," he said thoughtfully. "It looks like I'll have to show you how wrong you are."

The way he was looking at her made her shiver with awareness, and she stepped back again. He came after her. His hands reached out and he drew her into his arms, his hold on her firm enough to keep her where he wanted her, but not tight enough to hurt her. If she really wanted to, she could break away from him, but she didn't even try.

The world tilted when his mouth covered hers, hard and hungry. She was swamped with need, a whirlpool of sensations pulling her under as he parted her lips with his. His natural aggression was in every taut line of his body as he molded her slender form to his. She was the tinder and he was the spark. Between them they created a blazing fire that threatened to engulf them as Alex deepened the kiss.

Joanna knew this was why she had tried to keep him at a distance. Her response to him was instinctive and frightening in its intensity, overpowering her senses until all she was aware of was Alex. She was too vulnerable to contend with the sensual demands he could make on her.

Sensing her fear, Alex held a tight rein on his control. The bed was only a foot away, too close, too tempting . . . and too soon. He eased her arms from around his neck, holding her wrists as he lowered her hands, but he didn't move away from her. His resolution to stop while he still could was almost forgotten when she slowly opened her eyes, and he saw the sensual warmth in their dark depths. His fingers tightened around the fine bones of her wrists in an attempt to hold onto his control.

"Any questions?" he asked, his voice raw with restraint and desire.

She shook her head. There was a strange catch in her own voice as she murmured, "The only thing you've proven is it would be . . . interesting if we got involved, not that we will."

He raised a brow at her description. Interesting,

hell. Interesting was too tame a word for what they would do to each other and together. "It's too late, Joanna. I'm involved with you from your tapping foot to your dark silky hair."

Her frown reflected her confusion. She could argue from now until Sunday, except she would lose the argument if he decided to prove his point the way he had a moment ago. Just thinking about the riot of feelings he had roused deep inside her was sending tingles of awareness and heat through her.

"Pack your things and let's get this over with," she said wearily.

Alex hesitated. Knowing she returned his desire was different from wondering if he was the only one feeling this desperate craving. Her response had turned his body into a throbbing ache, but he wasn't about to ruin the progress he had made by rushing her into bed. He found he wanted her trust as well as her passion.

He slowly released her and walked over to the luggage rack in front of the small window. He shut his suitcase, snapping the clasps with a decided click. As he straightened he happened to look out the window. He stared down at the street for a long moment.

"Your boyfriend's followed us," he said quietly.

"What boyfriend?"

"Canfield. He's parked across the street in front of the ironmongers, but I doubt he's interested in purchasing any hardware at the moment."

Joanna walked over to the window and looked down. The familiar tan car was indeed parked at the curb, and Steven Canfield was sitting behind the wheel, gazing toward the hotel. "Why is he following us?"

"I imagine he's waiting to find you alone. Perhaps to give you a message from Travis."

She started toward the door. "I'll go down and see what he has to say."

Alex stopped her. "No. We wait for Travis to contact you personally. If Canfield has been sent by your brother, he won't tell us where Travis is."

"We won't know that for sure unless we ask him. Why make everything so complicated? I could go down and ask him point-blank what he wants. Maybe I wouldn't learn where Travis is, but it's becoming irritating to have him pop up wherever I go."

"I want you to stay away from him. It will be safer for you if Canfield continues to follow you at a distance."

Something had been bothering her, and she decided now was as good a time as any to find out the answer. "I don't understand why you are simply waiting around for Travis to contact me. You don't impress me as a particularly patient man. I would think you would be searching his apartment, talking to the people he knows, trying to find him at the various places he's known to go. You're wasting your time sitting around here. He may have changed his plans and won't be contacting me at all."

He kept his expression blank, giving none of his feelings or thoughts away. All the things she had mentioned had already been done without any success.

When he didn't speak, Joanna threw up her hands. "Never mind. You're going to do things your way no matter what I say. Don't treat me like someone who has a brain in her head. Just keep giving me orders. Who knows? I might even obey them."

"Hold it." He took her hand and drew her over to the bed. "Sit down."

"Why?"

"You've made your point." He paused for a moment, then added, "I expected you to take everything I say on trust, but I haven't given you much reason to do so. I'm going to tell you as much as I can."

She sat down.

"A group of computer experts working for the government have developed new, sophisticated programs to be used for satellite surveillance. The work is still in the experimental stages, so national security isn't involved. Travis has taken one of the most vital microchips. It still isn't clear how he managed to get past security in the building where the group was working, and it really doesn't matter at this point. What's important is getting the microchip back. Your father phoned me after making a deal with the government. I have two weeks to find Travis and get back the microchip. If I don't, government agents will be called in."

"How did my father know it was Travis who took the chip?" She answered her own question. "The note he left, right?"

"The case containing the rest of the microchips was left in the safe in your father's house in Georgetown, along with a note from Travis saying he had taken one of the chips. He also said he would be using you as a mediator."

She frowned. "When did all this happen?"

"About a week ago. Why?"

"Something doesn't make sense. Travis came to my office in Seattle a week ago, but he didn't say anything then about wanting me to act as a mediator."

"Why did he come to see you?"

"He told me he had something he thought I should see. He had found my birth certificate in Dad's safe, and he showed it to me."

"Why?"

She met his gaze. "The name of my father on the birth certificate wasn't Franklyn Kerr. My father was Stuart Kerr." She told him briefly about her real father's death in a climbing accident and how Franklyn Kerr had married her mother when he discovered she was pregnant.

Alex sat down beside her. "Is that why you came to see your grandmother?"

She nodded. "I needed to know what happened before I was born. I've lived a quarter of a century believing I knew exactly who I was. It was a shock to discover I'm not that person after all." She smiled wanly. "It's taking me a little time to adjust."

Alex stared at her. He was astounded by what she had just told him. It was the last thing he had expected. He admired her attitude. He wasn't sure he would be able to handle such a revelation as well as she was.

"Alex," she said, "I was in Washington four days ago. Why didn't my father tell me about Travis?"

"He wanted to keep you out of it if he could. After you came here to England, he realized he couldn't."

"And that's why he sent you after me, to be here when Travis contacts me."

"I think he was hoping Travis was playing some sort of game and would return the chip on his own. When he didn't, Franklyn called me. I'm not officially connected with the government anymore, and I can investigate without having to go through channels."

Joanna looked at him carefully. He sounded so matter-of-fact, as though traveling halfway around the world the instant Senator Kerr asked him to was perfectly normal. It was ironic that her father could count on this man when he wasn't able to rely on his own son's loyalty. She got off the bed and walked over to the window. The tan car was still there. "I realize I'm an amateur at this, but wouldn't it be easier to confront Canfield and see what he has to say?"

Alex picked up his suitcase and headed toward the door. "We'll let Canfield keep following us. At least we'll know where he is."

Joanna glanced at his case. It occurred to her he hadn't gone to the wardrobe or dresser before closing the lid of his suitcase. "You pack very quickly."

His hand on the doorlatch, he looked back at her. "I never unpacked."

She wasn't pleased with his answer and her expression made her feelings clear. "You expected to be invited to stay at my grandmother's all along, didn't you?"

Alex looked down at her feet, but they were both planted firmly on the floor. Apparently she was only mildly irritated, not toe-tapping angry. Hoping he was gauging her temper correctly, he said, "The invitation from your grandmother was totally unexpected. The reason my suitcase is already packed is because I never bothered unpacking. It's just as easy to live out of a suitcase."

It was as good an explanation as any, Joanna thought, but she still wasn't convinced he hadn't engineered the invitation out of her grandmother somehow. There was nothing she could do about it, though, so she figured she might as well accept it. It was her grandmother's home and her decision as to who would be her guest. The surprising thing was her choice in this instance had been Alex Tanner.

She preceded Alex out of the room, determined to get through the next couple of days without doing anything incredibly stupid.

Canfield's Cortina stayed far behind Alex's Jaguar during the drive back to Chesham. When Alex turned into the lane leading to Larksridge House, Canfield drove on.

The call Alex had made to Richard Sanders in London the night before hadn't produced any information on Steven Canfield, but the British agent had promised to keep digging. Canfield could be what he seemed, a man interested in making time with a woman, but Alex didn't think so. He could find it easy enough to believe the other man was attracted to Joanna, but his instincts told him Canfield's persistence was due to something else.

While Canfield watched them, Alex would be watching Canfield.

Joanna led Alex up the curved staircase to the guest room Elizabeth had chosen for him. The furnishings were similar to her own bedroom—a dark walnut dresser, chest, and a tall wardrobe that served as a closet. The oak floors and mahogany furniture were polished to a high sheen, and gave off a pleasant glow. A small fireplace was set into one wall with a black marble hearth and delft tiled front. The most impressive piece of furniture, though, was a massive bed complete with a canopy and side curtains.

The instant Alex stepped into the room, Joanna saw his gaze trail over the brocade canopy and the matching curtains tied back with tasseled cords.

To draw his attention away from the bed, she opened a door on the far wall. "This is the bathroom. You won't have to walk down the hall as you did at the hotel."

Alex set down his suitcase and came over to look into the bathroom. Standing beside her in the open doorway, he glanced inside. "A heated towel rack, wall heater, and shower. All the comforts of home." He spied another door opposite the one Joanna had opened. "Where does that door lead?"

She mumbled the next little bit of information. "It's my bedroom. You have to share the bathroom with me."

He slowly turned to look down at her, placing his hand on the door frame behind her head. "Your room is next to mine?"

He was too close, she thought nervously. The scent of his after-shave and the warmth emanating from his body were muddling her judgment, making her think of the intimate stroking of his tongue against hers when he had kissed her. Heat coursed through her and tinted her skin.

In an attempt to bring her mind and body under control, she said with forced lightness, "Guess whose idea it was to put you in the bedroom next to mine?"

"I would like to think it was yours, but that's too much to hope for." Bringing his other hand up, he touched the soft lock of hair laying over her shoulder. "I doubt if Stella even wanted me in the same house with you, much less sharing a bathroom, so that leaves your grandmother."

Joanna's lips parted as she was about to tell him he was right, but he was lowering his head. A soft sigh escaped into his mouth as he kissed her. The last thing on her mind was rejecting him. It would be easier to stop breathing than to turn down this chance to relive the magic he could create in her.

Alex held himself away from her by leaning on his hand pressed against the door frame. Allowing himself the luxury of her sweet lips, he didn't dare put his hands on her. He wouldn't be able to stop with tasting only her mouth if he did. The desire to sample the rest of her had him raising his head, breaking contact with her hot, satisfying mouth before he forgot where they were.

Moving away from her abruptly, he walked over to the bed and touched the curtain tied back to a bedpost, drawing the brocade material through his fingers. "Is your bed like this one?"

Joanna leaned back against the door frame. Her legs were too shaky to support her. She struggled to keep her voice casual. "If you mean does it have a canopy, then yes, it's like yours."

He sat down on the edge of the bed and tested the mattress with his hand. "Is your bed as comfortable as this one?"

"I don't know. I've never slept in this one." She walked over to the chest at the foot of the bed. "There are extra blankets in here if you need them. The nights are cool and the central heating isn't very efficient."

"There are other ways of staying warm than blankets."

His provocative remark brought her eyes to his, and she smiled faintly. "I'm sure I could find a hot water bottle for you."

"That's not quite what I had in mind," he murmured.

She didn't look away for a long moment, then she moved to the window to pull open the drapes. His words conjured up pictures of the two of them on the antique bed, her imagination fueled by the passion he had already stoked in her. Desire still throbbed deep inside her, and she knew she had to control it before she made a complete fool of herself.

Alex let his gaze follow her. Her grace as she did the simplest task intensified his attraction. If they weren't in Elizabeth Montain's home, he would be tempted to show her exactly how hot it could get in that bed. The thought of making love to her strained his control and the fit of his jeans, and he forced his mind back to the original reason for his visit. "Tell me about your relationship with your brother."

She glanced at him over her shoulder. "What do you want to know?"

"Why does he think he can count on you to cooperate with him? From what your father told me, you and your brother have never been particularly close."

She looked back out the window. "Travis may think I owe him a favor in return for the one he thought he had done for me by telling me who my father really was." She slowly turned around and met Alex's gaze. "He's wrong. I don't owe him anything. He didn't do me any favor."

Alex stared at her long and hard. "But he thinks you would be on his side rather than your father's?"

"Travis might think that."

"Would he be right?"

"No. Franklyn Kerr is the only father I've ever known. He deserves my loyalty and my love. I just wish he had told me before about my real father." She smiled. "I never even thought to question why

he always arranged for my passport and took care of
other documents that needed a birth certificate."

"You apparently have a close relationship with your
father, but you don't with your brother. Why?"

"I've always thought Travis felt he had to prove
something. Having a powerful father whom people
respected was a hard act for him to live up to, especially since his personality is the exact opposite of
Dad's. Travis always likes to be the center of attention and he does some bizarre things in order to get
it. He's gotten into a number of scrapes in high
school and college."

"What kind of trouble?"

"I don't know any specifics other than what my
father occasionally tells me. I was away at college for
four years and I've been in Seattle for two. I haven't
spent much time with Travis in a long while."

Before he could probe any further, they both heard
a distant knock. It was too faint to be at Alex's door,
but close enough to be someone knocking on Joanna's bedroom next door.

She closed her eyes briefly. "Oh, great," she
muttered.

"What's wrong?"

"What do you bet that's Stella pounding on my
bedroom door?"

He noticed she didn't seem overjoyed with the
prospect. "It could be your grandmother."

Joanna shook her head. "My grandmother rarely
comes upstairs due to her arthritis. Even if she did,
she wouldn't be any happier to find me in here than
Stella will be."

She started toward his door. "When she sees I'm
in here alone with you with the door closed, I'm in
for a royal scolding about proper behavior."

She opened the door and called out with resignation, "I'm in here, Stella."

Alex could hear the horrified gasp from where he sat on the bed. Joanna apparently knew what she was talking about. "I'll tell Stella it was my idea," he said.

"Thanks, but I fight my own battles."

The housekeeper's imposing figure appeared in the doorway, her hands clamped on her hips, her expression glowering in outrage. "You were to show Mr. Tanner to his room, Miss Joanna," she said in a low voice. "That is as far as our hospitality is to be extended."

Alex felt the housekeeper's displeasure when she directed her scathing glance at him. "Dinner is at eight," she said frostily, "with drinks in the drawing room at seven-thirty." Her gaze ran over him. "Mrs. Montain prefers to dress for dinner, Mr. Tanner, so do try to wear something more appropriate than those blue jeans."

Then it was Joanna's turn again. "We will not discuss this with your grandmother, Miss Joanna. I've come up here for the purpose of telling you there is a telephone call from the States and—"

Stella was left sputtering to an empty room. Alex had jumped up from the bed and followed Joanna as she ran down the stairs. She went directly to the sitting room; the receiver was resting on the desk. Joanna walked slowly to the desk, sat down in the chair, and picked up the receiver.

Alex took several steps into the study, his gaze on Joanna. Since Joanna's side of the conversation consisted of an occasional yes and one abrupt no, he had no idea what was being said. Abruptly, Joanna held the phone out to him. "He wants to talk to you."

He stared at her as he approached the desk. Taking the phone from her, he wondered what in hell was going on. He said his name and waited.

The male voice on the other end of the line was familiar. "According to Joanna," Franklyn Kerr said, "Travis hasn't contacted her yet. My sources still haven't turned up anything. Travis seems to have disappeared off the face of the earth. We're running out of time, Alex. Something has to be done and soon."

"I'm going to give him a couple more days," Alex answered. "There's another route I can take then if nothing develops here." Because Elizabeth entered the room at that moment, he didn't say anything more.

Something changed in the senator's voice as he asked, "Is Joanna all right? She says she is but I need to know what you think."

Alex drew his gaze to Joanna's face, aware of the shadows dimming her eyes as she returned his stare. "She's fine."

There was a decided weariness in the senator's voice as he said, "I realize Elizabeth is in the room with you so you can't speak freely. I was pleased when she told me you were staying at the house with them. I don't think Travis will try anything stupid, but then I didn't think he would steal from the government either. I feel better knowing you're there just in case Travis does attempt to contact Joanna."

Since there was nothing Alex could say in front of Joanna's grandmother, he remained silent. After a pause, Franklyn asked him to phone when he had any information, then hung up.

As soon as Alex put down the phone, Elizabeth said, "Stella told me Franklyn was on the telephone. I didn't realize you knew him, Alex."

"I met him in Houston when he was campaigning for the senate," he said. That was at least partly true.

Elizabeth smiled. "How nice. It is indeed a small world." Turning to her granddaughter, she said, "Isn't it nice you have something in common with Alex, dear?"

Alex was pleased to see amusement in Joanna's eyes. Her grandmother's matchmaking efforts were taking her mind away from worries about Travis. The only problem he had with that was he didn't think being paired off with Joanna was all that amusing. There was nothing remotely funny about the way she made him feel. He continued to look at her. When she met his gaze, desire whipped like a live current between them, arcing in the air around them.

He was startled when Elizabeth spoke again. "Were you involved in politics in Houston when you met Franklyn?"

He tore his gaze away from Joanna. "Not directly, no."

Elizabeth walked further into the room. "What an interesting life you must lead, Alex. You must tell us all about how you made the transition from a ranch to the world of politicians." She paused in front of the desk and looked down at Joanna. "We'll have tea in the drawing room, dear. I feel we could use a cup."

"Tea sounds lovely," Joanna said. "We'll join you in a moment."

Elizabeth smiled, obviously pleased that Joanna wanted to be alone with her new houseguest. "Fine. I'll have Stella bring the tea in fifteen minutes. Or would thirty be better?"

Joanna shook her head. "We'll be with you in just a few minutes."

Smiling brightly at them both, Elizabeth left the study.

As soon as her grandmother closed the door, Joanna said, "Evasive answers may have worked this time, Alex, but eventually you're going to have to tell her something."

"I'll tell her the truth."

"Not about Travis," she said strongly. "I don't want her upset."

Alex half-sat on the edge of the desk. "I'll only answer her questions about me."

He lifted her chin with his hand so she was forced to look at him. "I won't hurt her." His thumb stroked her bottom lip. "Or you."

Four

Joanna should have been able to sleep. The bed was comfortable and she was tired, but her eyes refused to close and her mind wouldn't allow her to slip into the oblivion of sleep.

Thoughts of Alex kept intruding no matter how she tried to push them away. During dinner, he had sat across from her at the refectory table. Elizabeth sat at the end, expertly guiding the conversation.

It was Alex's answers to her questions that were keeping Joanna awake.

As Joanna had expected, Elizabeth returned to the subject of how Alex had become acquainted with Franklyn Kerr. To Joanna's surprise, Alex openly admitted he had been a security agent at the time, and that he had been assigned to protect the senator after a threat had been made against Franklyn's life during a brief visit to Houston. The second night he was there, Franklyn met Alex's brother when Eric came to have dinner with Alex. Before the evening was over, Franklyn had accepted Eric's invitation to spend a weekend on the ranch. During that weekend, Alex became better acquainted with Franklyn, and the two men learned to respect each other.

It was the first of many weekends Franklyn spent at the ranch whenever he could find a gap in his campaign schedule. After he was elected, he asked Alex to head his security team in Washington, but by then Alex was ready to leave the world of investigation and protection behind. The appeal of danger, the excitement, the traveling had lost their attraction. He packed his gun away and never looked back.

When Elizabeth asked Alex why he hadn't returned to the ranch, he replied that he had wanted something different from the life he had had growing up. Besides, by that time several of his older brothers had married and had children. The ranch couldn't support an unlimited number of people. Everyone except Eric and two other brothers had gone into different occupations.

A faint scraping sound brought Joanna back from her thoughts. At first, she thought it must be her imagination, but then she heard it again. Her window overlooked the tiled roof of the garage. There were no trees close enough to that end of the house to make the grating noise against either that roof or her window.

She tossed back her covers and quietly walked over to the window. She pushed back the drapes. A quarter-moon gave off just enough illumination for her to see the outline of part of the garage and the driveway leading to it. She didn't notice anything out of the ordinary. Then a shadow flitted across the gravel drive.

She strained to see the front of the garage. One of the doors was partially open.

She saw the shadow again. It was too narrow and elongated to be one of her grandmother's dogs, and they slept inside anyway. The silhouetted outline of a ladder emerged from the garage, and her heart thudded loudly in her chest. She didn't move until she saw the shadowy form prop the ladder against the house, directly under her window.

Dropping the drape, she hurried across the room to the bathroom. Without thinking about her actions, she opened the door and strode through the bathroom into Alex's bedroom.

He was lying on his stomach, one arm sprawled out across a pillow. The sheet and quilt had fallen to just above his waist, exposing the bare expanse of his back.

She shook his shoulder. "Alex," she called in a loud whisper. "Wake up."

He rolled over, instantly awake. "What's wrong?"

"There's somebody outside my window."

He didn't ask any further questions. He tossed the covers back and sprang out of bed. Joanna was so preoccupied with the midnight intruder, the fact that he didn't have a stitch on didn't faze her as she impatiently waited for him to pull on a pair of jeans.

"Hurry up," she whispered urgently.

"I prefer to catch burglars with my pants on, if you don't mind. And in case you haven't noticed, it's about forty degrees in here."

She tugged at his arm. "All right. You've got your pants on. Let's go."

He brought his face close to hers. "You aren't going anywhere. You stay here."

"It's my bedroom."

"It's my sanity." With his hands on her waist, he picked her up and plunked her down in the middle of his bed. "You stay here."

On her knees, she moved to one of the bedposts and wrapped her hands around it as he disappeared into the bathroom. Straining her ears and eyes, she tried to visualize what was going on. But she couldn't hear a thing, and she certainly couldn't see anything in the darkened room. Being left alone with her fears and imagination was worse than confronting whoever was attempting to get into her grandmother's house.

There was nothing. No footsteps, no breaking glass, no sounds of struggle. This waiting was driving her crazy.

She had no idea what time it was or how many minutes had passed since Alex had left the bedroom. She told herself if he hadn't returned by the time she counted to one hundred, she was going into her bedroom. Flopping onto her back, she counted under her breath as she stared up at the canopy.

She had gotten to seventy-two when the mattress dipped slightly. Startled, she began to roll off the bed in the opposite direction, but was stopped by a hand on her hip.

"It's only me."

Relief flowed through her like a tidal wave. Collapsing back onto the bed, she gasped, "You scared me to death."

The mattress shifted again as he leaned over to turn on the small table lamp next to the bed. In the soft glow, he could see Joanna clearly, and he caught his breath. All she was wearing was a white cotton gauze gown with long sleeves. The ruffled neckline dipped in front, and a narrow pink ribbon closed the gap between her breasts. Her brown hair was mussed and tousled, and looked almost black spread out on the white pillowcase.

His hand was still on her hip, and he could feel her body shaking. Thinking she was cold, he flicked one of the blankets over her. "You'll be warm in a minute."

This was ridiculous, she thought. She couldn't stop shaking. He was safe, but she still couldn't stop trembling. "I'm not cold. This is just a reaction from being scared."

"There's no need to be frightened any longer. Whoever it was fled when I opened the window." He smiled. "The guy is going to be sitting carefully for the next couple of days. He was halfway up the ladder and lost his footing when he saw the window opening. I doubt if he saw me, but he might have been afraid you would call out and wake the others in the house." He chuckled. "When he fell, he landed on his butt."

"Do you think it was Canfield?"

"I wouldn't be surprised. He's seen us together, so he probably figures he doesn't stand a chance of talking to you during the day. He evidently thought he would climb into your bedroom in order to get you alone. It's a good sign."

She thought that was an odd way of looking at the attempted break-in. "Why do you say that?"

"It could mean Travis is getting impatient. Instead of using the phone to contact you, he wants Canfield to do it in person. Hey. You're still shaking. Relax. Canfield's long gone by now."

Her fingers fidgeted with the satin edge of the blanket. "I wasn't worried about Canfield."

He leaned over her, resting his hand on the bed, next to her hip. The gesture was curiously intimate, although he wasn't actually touching her. "Then why are you shaking? You said a moment ago you were scared."

Keeping her gaze on her fingers, she mumbled her answer.

He bent down. "You'll have to repeat that. I didn't hear you."

She raised her head, and her gaze collided with his. "I was worried about you," she said in a louder voice, sounding furious.

Alex stared down at her. Shock quivered through him. He could see the sincerity under the anger darkening her eyes. Maybe she had been concerned about him, but she didn't seem to want to be. An odd tug in his chest made him frown in bewilderment. What in hell was wrong with him? he asked himself. Did he actually like having her worrying about him? The answer came easily. Yes. He liked the thought of Joanna being concerned about him, because in order to fear for his safety she had to care what happened to him. She had to care for him.

Bringing his hand up to touch her face, he was startled to see his fingers trembling slightly. "Joanna," he murmured, needing to say her name. "I've been in more dangerous situations than having one man climbing up a ladder. As you can see, I'm still here."

"I don't want to hear about them," she muttered. She didn't even want to think about the danger he might have been in when he had been an agent. She lifted her hand and smoothed it over the hair-roughened skin of his chest, hating the thought of a knife or a gun cutting and invading his flesh.

Her touch seared his skin and sent a torrent of need swirling along his bloodstream, heating and hardening his body. She was in his bed, lying where he had lain, her head on his pillow. A man could only take so much temptation, and Alex gave in to the fierce pull of desire.

Keeping his gaze locked with hers, he trailed his fingers lightly down her throat. He could feel the increased throbbing of her pulse as he passed over a vein in her neck.

Joanna found it incredibly difficult to breathe as she looked into his eyes. She recognized the signs of arousal in him, because they reflected her own. Her hand still stroked his muscular chest, then stopped suddenly when her sensitive fingers glided over a ridge of scar tissue on his left side.

He answered her silent question. "It was barbed wire, not a bullet." His flesh quivered as her forefinger traced the long scar line. A soft sound of arousal escaped from his throat. "Do you have any idea what you're doing to me, Joanna?"

She wasn't listening. The thought of sharp barbed wire ripping through his flesh tore at her, tightening her stomach in an attempt to ward off the pain. As though to heal the long ago cut, she caressed his side. "How did it happen?"

His attention was on the way her fingers were gliding over his skin, but he managed to answer. "Eric and I were stringing new wire at the ranch and one of the staples he pounded in worked itself loose. Before either of us knew what had happened, the wire had backlashed and coiled around my waist. I grabbed it with my leather gloves but not in time to stop the barbs from tearing across my left side." Her hand had stopped its stroking, but remained spread out over his rib cage. He added, "Accidents happen all the time on a ranch."

"You have to be more careful."

He looked at her curiously. She didn't say he should be careful, but that he had to be. "I don't work on the ranch any longer, remember?"

She dropped her hand and tugged at the blanket to throw it off. "I'd better return to my bedroom so you can get to sleep."

He didn't move out of her way, and his arm effectively blocked her attempt to sit up. "You're staying here tonight."

"What?" she muttered in a strangled voice.

"We'll trade rooms for the rest of the night in case Canfield is stupid enough to try a return trip back up the ladder." As though he was thinking aloud, he murmured, "Travis must have given him the layout of the house. How else would he know which bedroom was yours?"

"If you remove the ladder and lock the garage doors, Canfield would be discouraged from trying it again."

"I'll take the ladder down in the morning before Stella gets up. Is there anything you need from your bedroom?"

"No, I don't need anything."

Unable to resist, he combed his hand through her silken hair. "I do."

"What do you need?" Her voice sounded as though

it came from a long distance and Joanna realized she was hardly breathing.

"You." He gazed at the soft lock of hair he was winding around his finger. "I didn't realize how difficult it was going to be to try to sleep in this bed with you in the next room. I wanted you beside me with your hair spread out on the pillow, your body next to mine."

A faint smile curved her mouth and a glimmer of excitement flickered in her eyes. Slowly, softly, she said, "I'm here now."

Giving in to the need to feel her slender body along his, he sank down on the bed beside her, partially covering her. Clenching his fingers in her hair, he held her head still as he bent down to take her mouth with his. The impact of his hunger shook them both as his tongue surged into the tantalizing warmth of her mouth.

Her gown had edged up beneath his leg, baring her thigh. When his hand smoothed over her skin, her legs shifted restlessly. She closed her eyes as delicious sensations flowed along her veins. She shouldn't be there. She shouldn't be enjoying his touch. She shouldn't be responding. Her body felt both light and heavy, as though she were floating but unable to move. Her pleasure was heightened by Alex's hand moving from her thigh to the opening of her gown, untying the pink ribbon and sliding inside.

He lifted his head, needing to see her eyes as her breast filled his hand. Her mouth was moist from his, and her eyes glowed with heated passion as she looked up at him.

"Touch me," he murmured, his voice raw with longing.

Lifting her arms took an incredible amount of effort, but once her hands slid over his firm shoulders, they took on a life of their own. Suddenly she couldn't touch him enough.

Alex knew instantly that it had been a mistake for him to beg her to touch him. His control was slipping dangerously, and he took a deep shuddering breath, trying to hold on to his raging need to bury himself deep inside her. Somehow he had to slow down.

He withdrew his hand from her breast and abruptly tugged her gown down, then pushed himself away from her. He sat on the edge of the bed, his breathing rough and ragged.

The sudden loss of his weight and warmth left Joanna feeling adrift, as though she were a boat torn away from its mooring. In an attempt to make some kind of contact with him, she raised her hand to touch him, but he seemed to sense what she was about to do.

He sprang off the bed and took several steps away from her. "You'd better get some sleep," he muttered.

"What's wrong?"

He turned, and groaned silently. He shouldn't have looked at her. The front of her gown was open, the pink ribbon dangling over the curve of one breast. Her mouth was moist and swollen from his kisses, her eyes dark pools of seduction.

The hardest thing he ever had to do in his life was turn down the invitation of her body. "Nothing's wrong. That's the problem."

Propping herself up on an elbow, she said hesitantly, "I don't understand."

The sight of her gown gaping even farther made it

almost impossible for him to say what he had to say. "Joanna," he began, his voice rougher than he intended, his words brutal with truth. "If I stayed on that bed with you a moment longer, I wouldn't be going into your bedroom to sleep. I would be inside you, making love to you for the rest of the night. If we were anywhere else but your grandmother's house, I wouldn't have been able to stop from making love to you." His mouth curved in a rueful smile. "I know she wants us to become involved, but I doubt if she would approve of us sharing a bed under her roof."

Shocked, Joanna realized she hadn't given a thought to her grandmother or anyone else during the past half hour. The last thing she wanted to do was to give her grandmother any cause for regretting her visit. The older woman held strong Victorian values left over from a strict upbringing, and she had been greatly disturbed when her daughter, Joanna's mother, had become pregnant out of wedlock. Joanna knew her sudden visit had brought all of Elizabeth's past hurts to the present. The last thing her grandmother needed was to have her granddaughter behaving as her daughter had.

The descent from the height of passion was sudden and painful. Joanna lay on her back and stared up at the canopy. She knew Alex was right, but that didn't make it any easier for her body to accept the cold dash of reality. Maybe it was for the best, she told herself. Becoming intimate with Alex would complicate her life, and she didn't know if she could handle his return to Houston. Just because she was tempted to have an affair with a man didn't mean she actually had to have one. He wouldn't be easy to forget, and she would have to do just that once he left her. And he would leave her.

She felt his gaze on her and turned her head to look at him. "Do you still insist on exchanging bedrooms?"

Jamming his hands into the pockets of his jeans, Alex didn't trust himself to speak. He nodded abruptly while he fought with his baser instincts. He realized that being in her grandmother's house hadn't stopped him from taking what his body so badly wanted and needed. Sex with Joanna would be mind-blowing, yet he knew what he wanted from her was more than physical.

His spine stiffened and his stomach tightened as if in anticipation of a blow. Was he falling in love with her? he wondered frantically. Was that why he felt a possessive urge to protect her, to keep her safe?

Joanna saw his expression change and wondered what was wrong. The low light from the lamp didn't extend to where he was standing, and she again propped herself up on her elbow in order to see his face more clearly.

A slash of heat cut through Alex as the front of her gown shifted, exposing more of her tempting breast. Her parted lips were an open invitation to his mouth and tongue. Muttering good night to her, he turned sharply and left his bedroom, closing the door firmly behind him.

When Joanna heard the click of the latch, she rolled onto her side, staring at the wall. Nothing in her life had prepared her for the upheaval of the past week. She'd led a charmed life. The best schools, the career she wanted, no financial worries, good health. Her life had been running smoothly and un-eventfully until she had been knocked off balance by Travis's startling announcement of her birth.

And now there was Alex Tanner.

Eventually her tired body took over, and she fell into a deep sleep, her arms hugging the pillow where Alex's head had lain.

Dawn was beginning to lighten the sky when Joanna crawled out of bed and stumbled over to the closed bathroom door. Listening closely, she couldn't hear any sounds of activity, so she opened the door. The bathroom was empty and the other door was ajar. Moving silently on her bare feet, she approached the door to her bedroom and peeked around the corner.

Her bed was made, the covers neatly smoothed. The room was empty. It looked as though she wasn't the only one who was up early.

Returning to Alex's bedroom, she saw his suitcase was now on its side on the luggage rack, the top open. It gave her an odd feeling to know he had apparently come into the bedroom while she was asleep. Biting her bottom lip, she couldn't help wondering if he had watched her sleeping. If he had, what had he thought as he looked down at her?

By the time she had showered and dressed, it was a little after seven. Stella would be in the kitchen, preparing breakfast. Her grandmother would still be in bed, sipping the cup of tea Stella had brought to her. Where was Alex?

Slipping on a jacket, she went out the side door to see if he had removed the ladder. The cool morning air brushed against her warm face as she stepped around the corner of the house. The ladder was gone. The Jaguar was parked where Alex had left it, which meant he was around somewhere.

Dew hung heavily on the grass as she strolled into the back garden. She shoved her hands into her jacket pockets as she let her gaze roam over the carpet of colorful crocuses blooming in clusters near the shrubs that lined the stone wall. She had no desire to go back to the house just yet and be subjected to Stella's sharp tongue and keen eyes.

Without thinking about where she was walking, she ended up on the edge of the apple orchard. Because the tree limbs were bare except for the buds getting ready to bloom, she was able to see a man dressed in dark slacks and a leather jacket examining one of the trees several rows into the orchard. The collar of Alex's jacket was up around his neck and the slight morning breeze ruffled his dark hair as he studied a small branch.

She could see the darker patches of grass where his booted feet had pressed into the damp ground, and realized she had been following those tracks without being aware of what she was doing.

Quickly turning around before he saw her, she retreated to the stone path that led to a white gazebo nestled in a corner of the garden. She wasn't ready to meet Alex just yet. She needed to think about what had happened between them last night, to put her thoughts in some sort of order and perspective. The cushions on the built-in benches inside the hexagon-shaped gazebo were damp. She turned one over before sitting down with her legs stretched out in front of her.

The wooden lattice sides of the gazebo allowed air to flow through it. A wicker table was set in the middle with four matching chairs arranged around it. In warmer weather Elizabeth liked to have her afternoon tea served in the gazebo where she could enjoy the fresh air and flowers. Now it was cold and damp, but also private, and that was Joanna's main priority at the moment.

When Alex walked out of the orchard, he immediately spotted the smaller footprints mixed with his in the grass. His gaze followed the dark indentions, and in the distance he saw portions of a white building in the midst of shrubs. He remembered the gazebo Elizabeth had shown him when they had taken a walk around the grounds.

He hesitated, then finally gave in to the inevitable and followed the footprints to the gazebo. When he had gone into his bedroom earlier, he had intended only to get a change of clothing. Still, his gaze had been drawn irresistibly to the slender form on the bed. Her slumber had apparently been restless. The covers were rumpled and tossed every which way. Her gown had inched up and his hungry gaze followed the lovely length of a bare leg from ankle to shapely thigh. It took every ounce of control for him to turn away from her and open his suitcase.

Joanna was first aware of Alex when his shadow fell across her. Looking up, she saw his tall figure blocking the doorway.

"Good morning," she said quietly, politely.

"Good morning." He sat down beside her, so close his hip pressed against hers.

She attempted a stab at conversation. "I noticed you put the ladder away."

"It gave me something to do since I couldn't sleep anyway." He slanted a glance at her, as if it were all her fault he didn't sleep. Which it was. "The lock hadn't been broken on the garage door. Does your grandmother usually leave her doors unlocked?"

"Probably."

"Would Travis have keys to the house?"

"I doubt it." Her hands remained in her pockets and she kept her gaze on the toes of her shoes. "Do you think Canfield will try again?"

"If he's been sent by your brother to get a message to you, he'll try again. Travis knows the setup in your grandmother's house. There's only one phone in the whole house and Stella usually answers it. Your brother is trying a more direct way of getting in touch with you."

"Why is Travis playing these cat-and-mouse games, Alex?" she asked seriously. "Why doesn't he just tell my father what he wants? Dragging this whole mess out isn't accomplishing anything."

"I asked your father the same question."

"And what was his answer?"

"He didn't have one."

"Do you?"

"Not yet, but I will."

"I've been sitting here thinking about Travis. He's been in a lot of trouble over the years, but I thought they were just childhood pranks, rebellion against authority, that sort of thing. I never realized how disturbed he was."

"What he's done this time can't be classified as a juvenile bid for attention. He hasn't just bent a couple of rules. Your brother has broken the law."

"I wish I had tried harder to understand him. Maybe I could have helped him."

Alex looked at her, noting the sadness in her eyes. "Don't feel sorry for him, Joanna. He's old enough to know right from wrong."

She sighed. "I know. It's a shame though. He has

had so many chances and opportunities, and he's wasted all of them. I can't help wondering if there wasn't something I could have said or done to make a difference, to help him."

"Help him do what? We all make our choices of how we want to live. He's made his." Alex covered her hand resting on her thigh, lacing his fingers through hers. "Travis isn't your responsibility."

She gazed down at their joined hands. As inevitable as the sun rising and setting, desire flooded through her the moment he touched her.

She dragged her thoughts back to the reason Alex was in England. "What's going to happen to Travis when you eventually find him?"

"It depends on what kind of deal your father can make with the government. He's going to try for psychological treatment instead of criminal proceedings. A lot depends on whether or not the microchip is returned intact."

She turned her head toward him. "Isn't there anything we can do? This waiting around is driving me crazy."

He stood, drawing her up with him. "We can go see if Stella will give us a cup of coffee."

With a deep sigh, Joanna walked beside him back to the house.

Five

After they had breakfast, Joanna went to her grandmother's bedroom to see what the older woman's
plans were for the day.

It turned out Elizabeth was leaving Alex and Joanna to fend for themselves. She had a meeting to
attend for the Dog Rescue Society and suggested
Joanna take their houseguest around to several nurseries to check out orchard stock. If they had time,
Joanna could also go along with Alex to see the
people he had come to get the orchid cuttings from.

Joanna couldn't help smiling at her grandmother's subtle matchmaking scheme as she left her bedroom. Then her smile disappeared. If her grandmother
only knew how well she had succeeded . . . at least
with one of the pair.

Joanna didn't want to, but she had to face her
feelings now rather than later. She was involved
with Alex more than she wanted to be, more than

she ever thought she could be, more than she should be if she had any sense.

Feeling as apprehensive as Anne Boleyn must have felt while awaiting execution in the Tower of London, she went looking for Alex. She, too, was in danger of losing her head, although figuratively, not literally.

Alex was in the study. He was leaning back in the leather chair, his feet propped up on the mahogany desk while he listened to whoever was on the other end of the telephone. From his expression, he wasn't hearing what he wanted to hear.

Joanna walked over to the French doors and looked out over the back garden. Alex's part of the conversation was limited and abrupt, giving her no idea whom he was talking to or what was being discussed.

When he put the phone down, it was with a decided show of temper.

"Nothing," he growled. "Nada, zilch, zero, zip."

She smiled at his expression. Alex was running out of patience. "Don't tell me. Let me guess. Travis is still among the missing."

"He's among the vanished." He stood up and shoved his hands in his back pockets. "Let's do something," he said. He sounded restless and frustrated. "Go somewhere."

She was surprised his patience hadn't given out before now. "My grandmother suggested I take you around to several nurseries so you can pick out some new apple trees for the orchard."

"It's as good an excuse as any." He took her arm and pulled her along with him toward the study door. "Get your coat and we'll get out of here."

When Alex made up his mind to do something,

Joanna thought, it got done. During the next several hours, she felt as though she were swept along by a whirlwind. She walked up and down rows and rows of saplings stuck in pots, standing beside him as he examined branches and roots before rejecting the trees. They went to three different nurseries before he found exactly what he wanted.

As she watched him carefully checking every tree, she had to admit he was taking his promise to her grandmother seriously. There was a specific type of apple tree he wanted and he wouldn't settle for anything but the healthiest trees he could find. It was obvious he hadn't been idly wandering around the orchard earlier.

As he pointed out certain young saplings to a member of the nursery staff, Joanna reflected on this new side to Alex. Instead of simply offering to help her grandmother with the orchard as an excuse to stay in the same house with Joanna, he was actually following through and getting the orchard in shape. He could have made excuses to Elizabeth or delayed any actual work on the orchard, yet he hadn't.

Once the trees had been selected and arrangements had been made for them to be delivered to Larksridge House, Alex wanted to look around the greenhouse. The air inside was humid and fragrant with a mixture of earth and flowers. He inspected a variety of plants as they wandered along the platforms where the plants were arranged at waist level.

Her skin was feeling prickly under her sweater and wool slacks from the hot moist air in the greenhouse. She decided to step outside for a moment.

Alex had struck up a conversation with one of the men who worked at the nursery, and she didn't bother interrupting them to tell him where she was going.

Outside, she shivered at the abrupt change in temperature from cloying warmth to brisk cold. Gravel crunched under her feet as she walked past tall laurel shrubs in large pots.

Suddenly, her arm was gripped tightly, and she was pulled into a cluster of shrubs. She started to cry out, but a hand clamped over her mouth, effectively cutting off any sound.

Her eyes widened with shock as she looked up and saw the face of the man who had his hand over her mouth. It was Canfield.

"Don't make a sound," he snarled, "and don't do anything stupid. I'm going to take my hand away from your mouth. If you scream for your boyfriend, I'll hurt you. Do you understand?"

She nodded several times. He removed his hand and watched her closely. His other hand still gripped her arm, hard and unrelenting.

"What do you want?" she asked.

"I have a message from Travis. He wants you to contact the senator. Today. Tell him he—"

"Angus." The woman's voice was close by. "Come look at these holly bushes."

Joanna had to bite her bottom lip to keep from crying out when Canfield tightened his hold on her arm. She heard gravel being crushed by heavy footsteps, then heard a man answering the woman.

Muttering under his breath, Canfield glared at Joanna and shoved her away. He disappeared among the shrubs.

Joanna took a few steadying breaths before emerging from the shrubs. A woman dressed in a wool plaid skirt and bulky sweater was standing next to a heavyset man. The woman was pointing to a clump of holly, but looked up when Joanna emerged from the shrubs.

Joanna smiled faintly at the couple and wondered how they would react if she thanked them. They would probably think she was nuts.

She was brushing laurel leaves off her sweater when Alex came out of the greenhouse.

"I've been looking for you." As he came closer, he saw the expression in her eyes. "What's wrong?"

She debated whether or not to tell him, then said, "I just had a run-in with Canfield."

"When?"

She gestured in the general direction of the laurel plants. "He said he had a message from Travis, but before he could say what it was, that couple over there scared him off."

Alex looked around but he didn't see Canfield anywhere. He turned back to her. "Are you all right?"

She flinched when he inadvertently grabbed her arm in the same spot Canfield had held her.

Alex loosened his hold. "You aren't all right. What did he do to you?"

"Nothing except pull me into the bushes."

He took her hand. "Come on," he said roughly. "Are we expected back at your grandmother's?"

She shook her head. "She has other plans."

"We'll stop someplace and have lunch then."

The nursery's car park had been full when they arrived, so Alex had parked across the street. They had to wait for several cars to pass before they could cross. As they neared the Jaguar, an old car came chugging along and the engine backfired as it passed them.

The sudden loud noise, so like a gunshot, didn't startle Joanna half as much as Alex pushing her against the car. He pinned her with an arm on either side of her, his body crushing hers into the door of the car.

Her hands automatically clamped onto his waist for balance, and she could feel the corded tension of his body. "Alex." Her voice was muffled against his chest. "It was only a car backfiring."

Covering her with his body had been a purely reflex action on Alex's part. The instant he heard the loud bang, his first instinct had been to protect her. Glancing to his left, he saw the smoky exhaust coming out of the back of the old car, the driver completely oblivious to the commotion his little car had caused.

Tension drained out of him, and he leaned heavily on his hands, still keeping her trapped between his body and the car. His extreme reaction had shocked him, and he needed a minute to pull himself together. He hadn't been concerned for himself but for Joanna. The possibility of her being in danger had galvanized him into action. If anything happened to her, he wouldn't be able to live with it.

Aside from feeling suffocated, Joanna was aware of every muscle and tendon in the hard male body pressing against hers. For some strange reason, she felt Alex needed comforting, although she couldn't imagine why. He wasn't the one who was squashed against a car with the door handle situated in an uncomfortable spot. She stroked his back but didn't try to push him away.

He moved back enough to see her face. "Are you all right?" he asked, his voice low and husky.

"Well . . ." she began hesitantly.

He grasped her shoulders. "What is it?"

"The door handle is stabbing me in the . . . behind."

Easing his body away from hers, he slid his hand down over her hip as though to erase any discomfort.

"Alex! We're on a public street. This is not the time to be fondling me."

He smiled slowly. "When *is* the time I can fondle you?"

"I'll let you know. You mentioned something about lunch."

He didn't want to eat lunch. He wanted to strip off her clothes and bury himself deep inside her. The need to make love to her had never been stronger, and he realized it wasn't only desire. He needed to feel her alive under him, reassuring him she was in no danger. The incident of the car backfiring had followed too closely behind her run-in with Canfield.

His arms went around her and he held her tightly against him. She slipped her own arms around him and allowed herself the luxury of filling her senses with his scent and the delicious feel of his warm body against hers.

A car passed by, and the driver honked his horn, either in approval or disapproval of seeing them embracing. Whatever the reason, the sound made them aware of where they were.

Alex drew away from her. She looked as dazed as he felt. "We'd better go."

"Where?"

"Lunch, remember?"

He helped her into the car, then slid behind the wheel and started the engine.

"Sorry about the lunge a moment ago," he murmured. "It was a knee-jerk reaction."

"Does that sort of thing happen often?"

He gave her a crooked smile. "At one time it happened too often, which is one of the reasons I got out of the security business. I was becoming paranoid. It was getting to the point where I was suspicious of the slightest bulge in a coat and would duck into a defensive crouch when a door slammed. I decided it wasn't worth it."

As he pulled away from the curb, she asked a question she had been wondering about. "Why did you get into the security business in the first place?"

He shrugged. "It seemed more exciting than working on a ranch."

"You thought people shooting at you was exciting?"

"My job was to keep other people from being shot. I was very good at it, but I decided it wasn't what I wanted to do the rest of my life. The waiting around was the worst part. The people I was guarding would be at a party or a meeting, and I would have to stand around until they were through. I discovered I liked growing things instead of guarding them."

She thought of how he had automatically blanketed her body with his own. "Was one of your job requirements to stand between a threat and the person you were guarding?"

He gave her a blank look, completely devoid of expression. "Yes."

She frowned, not liking the thought of how he could have stopped a bullet meant for whomever he was trying to protect. "You made a wise choice," she muttered. "People rarely get shot planting trees."

He smiled. "That's one of the attractions. The only enemies I've found so far in the landscape business are aphids."

Just ahead was a pub sign depicting two ornate golden keys crossed in the middle. "Have you ever been to the Crossed Keys Pub before?"

"No. All evidence to the contrary, I don't normally hang out in pubs when I visit my grandmother."

Alex parked the car, then turned to look at her, his expression serious. "But this isn't a normal visit, is it?"

"That's putting it mildly. The only thing normal is Stella's pots of tea and her grumbling."

He took her hand and rested it on his thigh. "This isn't normal. At least it isn't to me. All I have to do is touch you and I go up in flames." Loosening his grip on her hand, he spread her fingers over his hard thigh. "One of these days, I'm going to do something about it."

"One of these days, you're going to go back to Houston." She withdrew her hand. "Let's leave things the way they are."

"Which way is that?"

She heard the anger in his voice and looked at him. "Don't suddenly go dense on me, Alex. You know exactly what I mean. I'm having a few problems sorting out the relationships with my family as it is. I don't need any more problems. There are enough complications already."

"Honey," he said softly. "I have a feeling they're going to get a helluva lot more complicated."

With that cryptic remark, he got out of the car.

The interior of the pub was similar to the other one they had gone to the first day they met. Since it was lunchtime, almost every table was occupied, but they found a small one in a corner of the L-shaped room. There were no domino players, although several men in business suits were throwing darts at a board at one end of the room. A low mumble of conversation hung in the room and occasional bursts of laughter bounced off the plaster walls.

Alex elbowed his way to the bar and brought back a beer for himself and a lemon squash for Joanna. A young woman wearing a tight-fitting orange sweater that clashed with her flaming red hair came to take their lunch order. Joanna was amused that as far as the waitress was concerned, Alex was dining alone. She spoke only to him, smiling brightly.

Joanna watched the waitress sashay away. "Have I suddenly become invisible?" she asked Alex with amusement.

"Not as far as I'm concerned," he said, completely serious.

"The waitress doesn't agree with you."

He sipped his beer and leaned back in his chair. "Why haven't you ever married, Joanna?"

His sudden question took her by surprise. "I could ask you the same question."

He smiled lazily. "I asked you first."

"There hasn't been anyone I wanted to spend the rest of my life with."

Alex studied her while he thought about her simple answer. She hadn't said anything about love. Changing the subject again, he asked, "How did you get interested in speech therapy?"

She frowned. What was this? she wondered. Twenty questions? At least this one was easier to answer. "When I was in high school, a friend of mine had a speech defect. She was very pretty, blond, slim as a reed, but she rarely talked because she was self-conscious about her lisp. Unfortunately, her name was Lisa, which she had difficulty saying correctly. Whenever she was called on in class, she would die of embarrassment when some of her classmates giggled or snickered as she tried to answer the teacher's question."

"What happened to her?"

"One summer her parents sent her to a speech therapist. In the fall when Lisa came back to school, she was a different girl. She was more confident, more self-assured, spoke up in class, was asked out on dates. It was miraculous."

"And you decided you wanted to make those kind of miracles?"

She shook her head. "I don't make the miracles. The people who come to the clinic are responsible for their own miracles. They have to do all the work. I just show them various ways for them to go about it. Communication is important, vital to relationships, careers, and day-to-day living. There are a variety of reasons why people have difficulty communicating. Some are physical speech defects, some are psychological. I find it rewarding to be able to help people through therapy. Most of the time I'm successful."

•

The waitress chose that moment to serve their lunch, setting Alex's plate down gently and plunking Joanna's down with less grace. Much to the waitress's disappointment, Alex ignored her and the plate she had put in front of him. All of his concentration was on Joanna.

"Why Seattle?" he asked as the waitress left their table.

"The clinic there made me the best offer. It wasn't a hard choice to make since I always liked the area. In some ways Seattle weather reminds me of England."

"You didn't want to live closer to your family? Seattle is a long way from the capital." This time he wasn't surprised to see the shutters fall over her eyes. They came down every time her family was mentioned. Still, she didn't completely evade the subject as he expected.

"My father has been involved in politics a long time. After my mother died, he was rarely at home. It was as though he buried his grief in work. The house in Georgetown doesn't hold any particular childhood memories that would keep me going back like the ranch in Texas does for you. It isn't the ranch that keeps drawing you back, but your brothers and their families."

He had never thought of his trips back to the ranch in quite that way, but she was right. While she was still willing to answer his questions, he asked another one, "How old were you when your mother died?"

"Eight. Travis was three." She spoke without any emotion. "We had a succession of housekeepers over the years to take care of us while my father was carving himself a niche in the world of politics."

"Did you ever resent his preoccupation with politics?"

She thought about the question for a moment, then shook her head. "No. It's what he wants and he's done a wonderful job, accomplished a number of good things for the country. Why would I resent that?"

"Because politics took him away from home. You must have missed having a full-time father, especially when he was the only parent you had."

"It's difficult to miss what you've never had. I was used to him being gone. It couldn't have been easy for him either. He did make my graduation from high school and college, although he missed Travis's high school ceremony. That night Travis wrecked the car my father had arranged to be delivered for his graduation present. When Travis admitted he trashed the car on purpose, I asked him why he would do such a thing. He shrugged and said he didn't like the car."

Alex weighed everything she had said and came to the conclusion the distance between Joanna and her brother was apparently long-standing and more than just geographical. "I doubt if his father missing his graduation is the reason Travis has stolen the microchip."

Joanna leaned forward, her expression serious. "What if there were a number of incidents like that with Travis resenting Dad more and more? It might be one of the reasons he's gone to such extremes to get attention from him."

Alex had his own opinion. "I think it's more complicated. It could be that Travis would like to be like Franklyn Kerr, and he knows he never will be."

The waitress returned to their table, gushing concern when she saw Alex hadn't eaten his lunch. He hid his irritation as he assured the woman that the fish had been prepared perfectly. He just wasn't hungry.

"How about a sweet, luv?" the waitress persisted, and listed a selection of desserts as long as her bare arm.

Alex's gaze shifted from the waitress to a man standing at the other end of the bar. The man had been looking in their direction until Alex glanced at him, then he turned his back on their table, pretending an interest in his drink.

"Where's the ladies' room?" Alex asked.

A perplexed expression crossed the waitress's face. "It's toward the back past the saloon bar."

He asked her to wait a minute, then turned toward Joanna. "Go to the ladies' room," he ordered under his breath.

"I don't—"

"Go powder your nose or whatever for about ten minutes. Then meet me at the car."

"But—"

"Please do as I say for once, Joanna," he said softly. "I'll explain later."

Puzzled, Joanna stared at him for a long moment. Then she gathered her purse and pushed her chair back. There could be a variety of reasons why he wanted to get rid of her for a few minutes, but she hadn't the faintest idea what even one might be. Wanting time with the waitress wasn't one of them. She wasn't Alex's type.

Not that she knew what type of woman appealed

to Alex, Joanna thought as she pushed open the door to the ladies' loo. She washed her hands and spent the rest of the allotted ten minutes staring at her reflection in the mottled mirror hanging over the sink.

When she came out, another couple was seated at the table she and Alex had occupied. She walked through the crowded pub without rushing, which would have been difficult even if she had tried.

Alex wasn't waiting for her in the car or even near it. He was across the road about fifty yards away, down on one knee looking into a cardboard box. Completely mystified, Joanna hurried across the road toward him.

When she was a couple of feet away, she heard a strange noise coming from the box. "Alex? What's going on?"

He dipped his hand into the box and brought out a small brown bundle of fur. He turned slightly and held it out to her.

She clasped the squirming object in her hands. "Alex, this is a puppy."

He delved back into the box and brought out two more. "These are puppies too."

She knelt beside him and looked into the box. Two more puppies were nestled inside. "Do you think someone just dumped them here?"

"It looks like it."

"How did you know they were here?"

He put the puppies back into the box. "When I came out to the car to wait for you, I happened to glance across the street and I saw the box move. My curiosity got the better of me and I had to come check it out."

"What are you going to do with them? They can't stay here. They'll die."

"I haven't got that far. I've only just found them."

Joanna felt a warm, wet tongue stroking her wrist and glanced down. The puppy was licking her. She looked back up at Alex. "We'll take them home with us. Stella is going to raise the roof, but it can't be helped. We can't just leave them here."

"Doesn't she like dogs? There are four of them in the house."

"That's the problem. She likes them, but she thinks there're enough of them at the house already. She made my grandmother promise not to bring any more animals home." She handed him the puppy. "We'll have to figure out how to get past her."

He put the puppy back in the box. "How will your grandmother feel about having puppies in the house?"

"Right this minute, she is attending a luncheon and meeting of the Dog Rescue Society. She is against cruelty to animals, and"—she picked up the box— "this is cruelty to animals. Grandmother will know what to do with them."

"If we can get them past Stella."

That didn't pose as much of a problem as Alex thought it would. The kitchen was empty except for the four dogs. Stella and her shopping basket were gone. They only had to figure out what to do with the puppies until Elizabeth returned from her meeting, preferably without letting Stella know of their existence.

Alex set the box down on the table. The other dogs gathered around, sniffing at the box, but soon lost interest. "So where do we keep them until your grandmother gets home? Our room?"

Joanna almost dropped the puppy she had taken out of the box. "Our room?"

With the back of his forefinger, Alex stroked the small brown head peeking over Joanna's arm. "The room on the left at the top of the stairs where we've shared a bed. Technically, I used it the first half of the night, and you slept in it the last half of the night. It wasn't exactly the way I would have liked to share the bed with you."

Joanna's mouth went dry. The vision of being in bed with Alex was vivid in her mind and she felt her skin come alive as though he were caressing it. With effort, she pulled her thoughts back to the matter at hand. "Using your room might not be such a bad idea. Stella wouldn't go in there unless it was on fire. Maybe not even then. We'll keep them there until Grandmother comes home and we can decide what can be done with them."

Joanna heated some milk while Alex gathered up a saucer, several towels, and newspapers. When they had everything they thought they would need, they carried it all upstairs to the guest room. While Joanna lit the kindling that had already been laid in the fireplace, Alex covered the hearth rug with newspaper and lifted each puppy from the box.

The puppies needed a little coaxing to take the warm milk. Holding one in his lap, Alex dipped a finger into the milk and touched the small mouth. Eventually a little pink tongue came out and licked his finger. Each time he brought more milk to the puppy's mouth, he moved the puppy closer and closer to the saucer of milk, until the puppy finally learned what he had to do in order to get all the milk he wanted.

Joanna watched Alex, then tried the same procedure on a different puppy. It took patience and time, but their efforts paid off. Soon all five puppies were happily lapping up milk like pros.

Grinning broadly, Joanna lay on her side, propped up on one elbow, while she watched the puppies. "They were hungry."

Alex stretched out on the other side of the puppies. "In another couple of hours, they're going to be hungry again."

"So soon?"

He nodded. "They have tiny tummies but big appetites."

She glanced at her watch. "It's one o'clock now, so around three o'clock, I'll have to sneak some more milk out of the kitchen. You can keep Stella occupied somehow while I'm getting the milk."

He arranged a towel in the box and laid a drowsy puppy on it. "I'll get the milk and you keep Stella occupied."

"Don't tell me you're afraid of Stella? In your former line of work, you must have run into more formidable opponents than my grandmother's housekeeper."

"At the moment, I can't think of a single one."

Another puppy with a full tummy fell asleep and Alex settled it into the box too. Soon all five puppies were snoozing soundly.

"We make pretty good foster parents, if I do say so myself," Alex murmured.

Joanna sat up and wiped her hands on one of the towels. "Now that we have the children all settled," she said dryly, "how about telling me why you wanted me out of the way in the pub."

Amusement glittered in his eyes. "You aren't going to like it."

"Probably not, but tell me anyway."

He rolled onto his back, his hands pillowing his head, his booted feet crossed at the ankles. "Well," he began, "I didn't want you there when I offered the waitress ten pounds to do a favor for me."

Joanna had trouble following that simple sentence. Alex's long, lean body was relaxed and incredibly enticing as he lay sprawled out on the rug so close to her. She wet her dry lips with her tongue. "What was the favor?"

"I asked her to accidentally on purpose spill a pint of lager on a certain gentleman." He smiled as her mouth dropped open. "It's a shame you couldn't have seen it. She was an expert marksman. It made me wonder whether she'd done that sort of thing before. I had to pay for his drink since he left without paying, but it was worth it."

Joanna didn't know which question she wanted answered first, so she asked them both. "Who? Why?"

"Our friend Canfield had followed us again, and I decided to get rid of him for a while."

Slowly Joanna's bewilderment changed to genuine amusement. "What reason did you give the waitress for spilling the drink on him?"

He turned his head to look at her. "I told her we were having an illicit weekend and the guy at the bar was a private detective sent by your husband to follow us."

Joanna grinned. "And she believed you?"

"She's a romantic at heart." Suddenly he reached out and pulled her on top of him. "Speaking of romance." Her mouth opened to protest, but his soft laughter and warning stalled her. "Shh. You'll wake the babies."

With one hand at the back of her neck, he brought her head down to his. Desire was immediate, a stinging pleasure and pain. There was no testing or teasing, only primitive hunger made more potent by the times they had stopped short of satisfying the passion between them.

His hands slid down her back to cup her bottom, pressing her into his aroused body. She moaned softly into his mouth and, to ease the ache deep inside her, ground her hips against his.

"Joanna." He groaned against her lips, his need deep and raw. Rolling over with her, he reversed their positions. He invaded her mouth with his tongue while his hands roamed and stroked her writhing body. When one hand settled on the warm feminine mound between her legs, the soft mewing sounds deep in her throat nearly drove him over the edge.

Needing to feel her naked flesh, he pushed her sweater and shirt up and slid his hand over her rib cage. "Joanna, your skin is so soft, so hot. Like satin on fire."

Restless, searching for an end to the ache deep inside her, she twisted her legs around his. "Please," she breathed, not sure what she was pleading for, an end or a beginning.

"It's all right." His voice was hoarse and rough with need. "Just a few minutes more."

With a few swift movements, he took off her sweater, shirt, and bra, leaving her bare and exposed to his eyes and hands. For a few moments, he only looked at her breasts, the slender lines of her waist and her throat before lowering his mouth to taste her soft womanly flesh.

Darkness whirled around her as she closed her eyes against the primal pleasure jolting through her. Arching her back, she threaded her fingers through his hair to keep him at her breast. Her breath came in short gasps as she tried to pull badly needed air into her starving lungs.

It was too much, yet not enough.

The slamming of a door in the distance vibrated through the floor, but it took a few minutes for the significance of the sound to find its way through the passion.

Joanna suddenly froze. "Alex, Stella has returned."

Collapsing on her, he buried his face between her breasts as a shudder shook his whole body. He tortured himself by slowly dragging his throbbing body off her.

Resting his hand just below the slope of her breast, he said. "There will come a time when we won't be interrupted, when I won't be able to stop. We're going to have to do something about this and it's going to have to be soon."

She didn't want to talk about later. Her body was craving the satisfaction only he could give her. Knowing he was right didn't ease the desperate tension inside her.

Sighing heavily, she sat up and put on her bra. She had forgotten why Alex was in England. "It's going to have to be soon," he'd said. Soon, because he wasn't going to be there much longer. She slipped on her shirt and began to button it. She gave the sleeping puppies one last look, then rose to her feet.

"You stay here with them, and I'll go see if that was Stella or my grandmother who came in."

She picked up her sweater and turned. Alex caught a glimpse of the expression on her face, and it was enough to bring him to his feet. "Joanna, we have to talk about this. It won't just go away."

"No, it won't," she admitted. At the door she paused with her hand on the latch. "But you will."

Six

When her grandmother returned from her meeting, it was time for afternoon tea—which Elizabeth considered a necessity rather than a ritual. It was an hour before Joanna was able to speak to her alone and tell her about the puppies. Elizabeth insisted on seeing them, placating Stella by telling her the puppies would only be their guests temporarily. When Stella looked doubtful, Elizabeth only smiled and asked Joanna to bring down the puppies immediately.

Upstairs, Joanna found Alex standing by the window in his room, his hands shoved in his back pockets and a brooding expression on his face.

He turned when she spoke. "My grandmother wants to see the puppies."

"What about Stella?"

"Grandmother has promised her they won't be staying." She smiled faintly. "Grandmother thinks it's amusing that we've kept the puppies hidden in your room."

His sober eyes drilled into her. "I don't find anything remotely funny about this afternoon." He was extremely edgy, and had tried to put it down to sexual frustration, but he knew it was more than that.

Moving abruptly, he picked up the box full of snoozing puppies. "You get the rest of the things on the rug," he ordered roughly. "Let's get this over with."

He brushed by her and left the room, and she stared at the empty doorway. Her shoulders slumped wearily in defeat. It would have been nice if they could have parted as friends, even though they would never be lovers.

The tiny bundles of fur took center stage for the rest of the day and into the evening. To Stella's horror, all five puppies were allowed free rein on the drawing room carpet. She bustled around after them with towels, mopping up their ocassional accidents, and muttering under her breath.

While they were all feeding the puppies, Alex told Elizabeth about the trees he had ordered and when they would be delivered. He spoke only to the older woman, as if Joanna weren't in the room. Joanna, on the other hand, spoke mostly to the puppies, which under the circumstances was a one-way conversation at best.

The atmosphere worsened after a member of the Dog Rescue Society came for the puppies, who had provided a buffer, but once they were gone, the strain of maintaining normal conversation was obvious and uncomfortable.

After a few minutes of restless pacing, Alex excused himself and left the house. He started toward his car, but decided he wasn't in the mood to drive anywhere. He just needed to get away from Joanna.

Simply being in the same room with her was driving him crazy. He felt as tightly wound as a spring and he knew why. The problem was he didn't know what he was going to do about it.

Going around the side of the house, he walked toward the orchard. It was time to ask himself some serious questions and hope he could come up with the answers before he went out of his mind. What had happened to the single-mindedness that had made him successful in the past? he asked himself. His priority should be to find Travis. Waiting for something to happen wasn't working, so it was time to make something happen. It was time to put an end to this case and get back to Houston.

But what about Joanna?

"What about Alex, Joanna?"

"What about him?"

"He seemed a trifle upset about something. Did you two have an argument?"

She could pretend she didn't know what her grandmother was talking about, but she didn't even try. "Not exactly."

"Sometimes the paths we take to find happiness are rough. Occasionally we take the wrong ones, too, but I think Alex is the right path for you to take, Joanna."

Sitting in a chair across from her grandmother, Joanna gave her a crooked smile. "Or you wouldn't have invited him to be a houseguest?"

"I see I haven't been able to fool you." Elizabeth looked serene, without a trace of guilt. "I admit I had an ulterior motive in asking Alex to stay here while you're visiting me. I liked the cut of his cloth the minute I saw him."

Joanna hesitated for a moment, then said seriously, "Just because you may want something to happen doesn't mean it's going to happen."

"Oh, I wouldn't be so sure. I have eyes, darling. They may be old, but they can see two people who tried very hard not to look at each other this evening, yet were aware of every move the other made."

"I won't deny I'm attracted to him, but he will be gone soon. He lives in Houston and I live in Seattle. That's not exactly next door."

"You're talking geography, Joanna. Not love."

Joanna suddenly felt incredibly tired. "It's a little early to be discussing love, don't you think?"

"Is it?" Elizabeth asked softly.

Joanna didn't answer her grandmother's question then, but later she had to answer it to herself. She was either in love or she was coming down with something. If she was in love, it wasn't the way she thought she would feel. In books, movies, and songs, love made people deliriously happy. She was miserable.

Heaven help her, she was in love with Alex Tanner.

She sat on the padded window seat in her bedroom, looking down into the back garden. Her gaze followed the lone man walking on the outskirts of the orchard. Leaning her head against the cool glass, she wondered what he was doing, what he was thinking, and why he was staying outside so long. She couldn't help wondering if his thoughts were about her. About them.

She watched Alex's shadowy figure as he slowly strolled back toward the house. Instead of sitting there like some lovestruck teenager, she told herself, she had better decide what she was going to do. It was up to her how she lived her life and she had better get on with it. It was time to do something about resolving the situation with Travis, and then Alex could be on his way. Alone.

And she would go her way. Alone.

Early the next morning, Joanna showered quickly, then pulled on a pair of jeans and a bulky red sweater over a white shirt. While she was tying the laces of her running shoes, she heard the shower again running in the bathroom. Alex was also awake.

She ran lightly down the stairs and headed for the kitchen. Stella was doing her usual magic with scones and the teapot, a solid rock in the foundation of Larksridge House.

"Good morning, Stella."

Stella placed a folded cloth napkin on Elizabeth's tray. "Good morning. You're up early."

"I thought I would pack a lunch and go to the Abbey." She didn't mention that she hoped to draw Steven Canfield into following her. Stella might raise a ruckus and forbid her to go. Worse, the housekeeper might cause such a commotion, Alex would hear her. Joanna knew he would definitely try to stop her if he knew what she planned to do.

Stella made a disgruntled sound deep in her throat. "I don't know why you like those old ruins. They're just a pile of rubble and weeds."

Joanna took out a loaf of bread and cut two slices for her sandwich. "I like piles of rubble and weeds." Changing the subject quickly, she asked, "Would you like me to slice some bread for toast?"

"You might as well cut two slices for him," Stella muttered with a martyred air. "Is he going with you?"

"No, Stella," she answered patiently. "He won't be coming with me."

"Then what will he be doing? Your grandmother will be out all afternoon attending the hospital auxiliary meeting. I'm not going to entertain him."

Joanna placed a slice of ham and slivers of Leicester cheese between the two pieces of bread. "The trees he ordered yesterday for the orchard are supposed to be delivered sometime today. The nursery will be sending some men along to plant the trees, but Alex will probably supervise."

"As long as he isn't underfoot all day. Would you like a cup of tea before you go?"

Shaking her head, Joanna tucked the wrapped sandwich into the canvas carryall she had brought down with her. She didn't want to linger in the house any longer. Alex would have finished his shower by now and would soon be coming downstairs. She wanted Canfield to follow her, not Alex.

Stella filled a flask with hot tea, liberally laced with milk and sugar. She stuck it into Joanna's carryall, along with an apple she polished briefly with her apron. "Now be off with you," she said gruffly. "See that you mind where you're going. I don't have time to go looking for you if you get lost."

Smiling, Joanna kissed the housekeeper's cheek. "I'll be back by teatime."

She slung the carryall strap over her shoulder and let herself out the side door. The ruins were some distance from the house, hidden by a line of trees and hedges. The property the ruins were on had belonged to the Montain family at one time, but had been sold after Joanna's grandfather had died. Her grandmother hadn't wanted the responsibility of the extensive property or the taxes that went with it.

She could have walked through the orchard to the ruins, but she decided to take the long way around instead, up Chartridge Lane. She would be in full view of the street, so Canfield would see her if he was watching the house. There was no sign of a tan car anywhere when she walked through the gates and looked up and down Chartridge Lane. Just because she didn't see his car, though, didn't mean he wasn't keeping an eye on the house. She could only hope he hadn't given up. If he had a message from Travis, she was going to give him the opportunity to pass it on to her.

Turning up a narrow lane, she strolled alongside a white fence that ran the length of the lane to a long narrow building that had once been the Montain Stables. Elizabeth had passed on her love for horses to her daughter, Amelia, Joanna's mother, who had spent many hours jumping horses or riding over the extensive Montain property. Now the stables were leased to a woman who gave riding lessons and boarded other people's horses.

Gillian Prescott was exercising one of the horses as Joanna approached. Joanna had met Gillian several years ago and had accepted her invitation to ride any of the horses during her visit, an offer Joanna had taken advantage of whenever she came to visit her grandmother.

Gillian saw her standing by the paddock fence and waved. Lifting her hand in response, Joanna leaned her arms on the top board of the fence and watched Gillian ride toward her.

Stopping near the fence, Gillian smiled down at Joanna. "I was wondering if you were going to come for a ride while you were here."

Joanna stroked the velvet muzzle of the chestnut bay. "How did you know I was here?"

"You met my aunt last night. Your grandmother called her to come pick up some puppies. She told me you were visiting your grandmother."

"I keep forgetting what a small town this is."

"Did you want to ride this morning?"

Joanna shook her head. "Not today. I'm on my way to the Abbey."

The horse's head jerked up and down several times and Joanna dropped her hand. Gillian expertly quieted the horse as she looked down the lane to see what had disturbed the horse.

"One of us is going to have some company," Gillian said with amusement, "and I have a feeling it's you. Worse luck."

Slowly turning her head, Joanna saw Alex striding toward them. He was dressed in jeans, a black sweater, his usual western boots, and his leather jacket. His hands were jammed into the front pockets of the jeans. As he came closer, she noticed lines of exhaustion in his face, especially around his eyes, that hadn't been there before. Still, he was the most vital, virile man she had ever seen.

When he stopped beside her, she made the introductions. He acknowledged Gillian with a nod and reached out to stroke the side of the horse's proud head. The horse took exception to his touch and jerked his head away.

He spoke to the horse in a low crooning voice, gentling him with a mesmerizing tone until the spirited animal accepted his touch.

Gillian was impressed. "Pax usually doesn't like men. The man who owned him before used a whip on him."

"The man should be the one whipped," Alex said, using the same steady tone of voice so he didn't startle the horse. "This is a fine animal."

"Would you like to ride him? He could use a firm hand on his reins."

He shook his head. "Maybe some other time."

The horse was becoming impatient with the inactivity and began to scrape the ground with a front hoof. His rider smiled. "It was good to see you, Joanna. I hope you can find time to ride while you're here." Sliding a glance at Alex, she grinned. "But if you can't, I'll understand."

She turned the horse and trotted away. Joanna kept her gaze on them as she asked quietly, "How did you know where I was?"

"I saw you leave the house and followed you. Were you planning on going riding before I arrived?"

"I'm going to the Abbey." Dropping her hands from the fence, she looked behind him, but couldn't see anyone else in the lane. "Did you happen to see Canfield?"

"No. Was I supposed to?" His expression hardened. "Is that what this little romp in the country is all about? You're using yourself as bait to lure him out?"

"Something like that." Dark fire flashed in his eyes, and she added quickly, "If he has a message for me from Travis, I plan to give him the opportunity to pass it on to me. We have to get this mess settled, Alex. Waiting around isn't accomplishing anything."

Giving himself time to control his temper, Alex watched Gillian school the spirited horse. The odor of leather, straw, and horse were the familiar smells from his childhood, and brought back memories of an easier time in his life. The familiar earthy fragrances grounded him, gave him an equilibrium, a balance he had lost during the long sleepless night.

He looked back at Joanna. "All right. Let's go wherever you were going, and we'll make some plans. I don't want you stumbling into a meeting with Canfield without some safeguards in place."

As Joanna started toward the grove of trees, Alex fell into step beside her. Neither spoke as they walked. Joanna was relieved Alex was willing to do something about finding Travis, but being with him was a sublime torture.

The sound of hoofbeats was left behind as she took a narrow path leading into the trees. It wasn't long before they cleared the trees and entered a field of daffodils, their yellow blossoms brilliant and startling against the background of stubby brown grass.

Alex stopped and looked around. Straight ahead, he could see a stone wall rising from some shrubs, vines crawling up its side. Several large stones were laid out in broken rows, parts of another wall that had crumbled over the years.

"The Abbey?" he asked.

She nodded. "Around the twelfth century, this was a monastery for Benedictine nuns. I found it one day when I was about ten and asked my grandmother about it. She hadn't leased the stables then and I was allowed to ride here whenever I wanted."

"I didn't know you liked to ride horses."

She bent down and picked a daffodil. "You mean it wasn't in the report about me?"

Jerking his head around, he stared down at her. He could have denied any knowledge of a report, but decided it wasn't worth it. "There was no mention of horses or any other hobby."

She hadn't been sure there had been a report, yet wasn't surprised when he confirmed there was. "I know that's how things are done in the security world, and it's probably necessary in some cases, I don't like the idea of being spied on, though."

"Not too many people do."

"The report told you where I worked, where I lived, every aspect of my life. You knew everything about me before you even met me."

"Not everything," he said softly. "I didn't know I would want you so badly."

Startled by his blunt statement, she met his gaze. She could pretend she didn't know what he was talking about, but she had gone past the stage of denying there was anything between them.

She sighed heavily and looked at the flower she held in her hand. "It complicates things, doesn't it."

With his fingers under her chin, he lifted her head so she had to look at him. "It doesn't have to."

She took several steps away, needing distance between them. "It would and you know it. You have a job to do, to find Travis and get back this microchip he stole. Then you will be returning to Houston. I can't see where I fit into any of those plans, unless you're expecting to indulge in a brief affair." Her voice changed, no longer calm. "Is that what you want, Alex? A few hot nights with a woman who happens to be handy before you report mission accomplished and head back for the Lone Star State?"

He stood with his feet slightly apart, anger darkening his eyes to hard gray steel. "Are you through?" His voice was deadly quiet.

She took a deep breath and nodded.

Alex didn't touch her. He didn't dare. "I was doing a favor for your father when I came here. I had a job to do. That was all. I wasn't looking for a good time with his daughter as a bonus. I didn't expect to have my guts tied into knots when you walk into a room, or to lie awake at night aching to the soles of my feet because I want to make love to you. I can back off if that's what you want, but it will be the hardest thing I've ever had to do."

He was talking about the present, she thought, the moment, not the future. She couldn't tell him she wanted forever with him, because he wasn't offering forever. The only commitment he was making was for now.

She began to walk again, carefully stepping around the bright yellow heads of the daffodils. His patience running out, he took her arm. "Dammit, Joanna. Answer me. This isn't going to disappear by your simply walking away from it."

"I know." A faint smile containing more sadness than amusement curved her mouth. "I don't know if I can make you understand. I've learned not to depend on anyone but myself. It's not easy for me to relinquish control to someone else, and that's what's been happening since I met you. I find myself thinking about you when I should be thinking of other things. I wonder what you're thinking when I'm with you and what you're doing when I'm not with you. That's never happened to me before and it scares me silly."

Fear tugged at his stomach. "So what are you saying? That you want to play it safe and stay uninvolved?"

"It's too late for that. You said so yourself. We are involved. What I'm saying is that I would expect more from you than you're willing to give."

Anger blended with the fear. "Maybe I would surprise you."

"Maybe you would. I've never been much of a gambler, Alex, but I'm tempted to become one with you."

Feeling she needed some kind of reassurance from him, he said, "I'll take whatever you're willing to share and I'll give you back whatever I can."

He was making a commitment of sorts, she thought. Possibly the only kind he could make. The stakes were high and she might come out the loser, but she would never know unless she took the chance.

She lifted her hand and felt the warmth of his fingers as they closed around hers. "I'll show you the Abbey while we're here."

As they neared the ruins, Alex could see large foundation stones embedded in the ground, partially covered with moss and lichens. Three walls several feet thick were still joined at the corners, but without a roof. A large square of stone remained with weeds growing between the fitted stones. Stepping up onto the floor, he saw a large fireplace built into one of the walls, its chimney broken off. There were traces of half-burned logs resting in the cavernous fireplace, an indication that others enjoyed the ruins.

He felt as though the modern world had disappeared, and he and Joanna had been transported back to another time. The only sounds were several birds chatting in the trees and a slight breeze ruffling dry leaves on the stone floor.

Pulling her hand from his, Joanna walked over to the fireplace. She dropped her carryall onto the high stone hearth, then gathered a few small twigs and branches, and a handful of dried grass. After arranging them in the fireplace, she took a small box of matches out of her pocket, struck one, and lit the smaller twigs.

Alex picked up more wood and brought it over to the hearth. "Do you usually make a fire when you come here?"

"A fire makes the place cozy, don't you think?"

He couldn't help smiling at her tone of satisfaction.

She sat down on the wide hearth and looked around at the familiar ruins of the once-magnificent building. "Grandmother showed me drawings of how the Abbey looked long ago." She pointed to an area in the opposite direction from the field of daffodils. "There was a lake and several outbuildings over there. The Abbey wasn't very large, only two stories with twenty rooms. I asked my grandmother why it was allowed to fall into ruin, and she said it had been badly damaged during the civil war sieges in the mid-seventeenth century."

Alex sat down beside her. The twigs had caught and soon the larger logs would be burning. Feeling the warmth against his back, he realized he had just learned something new about Joanna. She was a dyed-in-the-wool romantic. "I think you prefer it this way," he said. "When you first found this place, did you spend hours here imagining a knight on a white horse riding up to carry you away?"

She didn't deny it. "Having an English mother and grandmother, I was raised on stories of knights in shining armor." She gave him a teasing smile. "In the same way I imagine you were raised with stories of cowboys and Indians."

He looked into her shining eyes, and thought he would be willing to slay a few dragons for her if she would smile at him like that again. "It's a shame there aren't any knights around anymore."

"Oh, but there are. Chivalry just comes in different forms these days. Instead of suits of armor, sometimes knights wear jeans and cowboy boots."

"Don't put me into the role of knight, Joanna. I'm the last man who would fit that mold."

"You were all set to protect me when you thought there was a gunshot yesterday when we were leaving the nursery, and you're trying to protect me now from Steven Canfield."

"About Canfield." He broke a branch in two before tossing both pieces into the fire. "I doubt if he'll be coming to the house again after his abortive attempt at climbing in your window. His grabbing you at the nursery could mean he's becoming impatient. What we need to do is give him an opportunity to talk to you where you'll be safe."

"How are we going to manage that?"

"We'll go out to dinner tonight. Your grandmother told me about a restaurant in Amersham called The Water Mill. It's a converted mill complete with a working paddle wheel. She said the tables are arranged in various sectioned-off parts of the mill, giving the patrons privacy. I have a feeling her reasons for telling me about the privacy was for the benefit of the romance she's hoping we're having."

Joanna let his last remark go by without comment. "Canfield won't come near me as long as I'm with you." Suddenly she had an idea. "I could go to the ladies' room. Maybe he'd use that opportunity to approach me."

Alex didn't like the way her eyes lit up with excitement, as though she was enjoying the cloak-and-dagger strategy. None of the possible dangers seemed to occur to her. He wasn't going to point out the risks, but he would tell her what they were going to do instead.

"I'll go to the men's room this time. I'll pretend to drink too much, which will make him feel more confident. You wait at the table for him to come to you. No matter what he says or does, you stay at the table. I'll be nearby."

"What if he says he can take me to Travis? Shouldn't I go with him? You could follow us."

He shook his head. "There are too many variables if you leave with him."

"It's just like Travis to get someone else to do his dirty work for him."

"If Canfield wants to talk to you, he'll have to come to you, and I can keep an eye on you in case he tries anything. This way we will be in control of the situation, not him."

Joanna paused, letting his words sink in. Then she asked, "You think Travis is getting impatient, don't you?"

"Your father told me Travis was weak in character

and stiff with pride. That's an unstable combination. I don't want you in the way if he's planning something stupid, like having Canfield kidnap you."

"Travis wouldn't hurt me, if that's what you're implying."

His voice hardened. "I'll make sure of it. Your brother has a king-size grudge against you and your father. I want you out of it completely."

"Why would Travis have a grudge against me? We may not be the best of friends, but he's never shown any animosity toward me."

"In the note to your father, Travis referred to you as 'Daddy's little girl.' I got the impression it was not an affectionate term." He cursed under his breath. "Your father should have seen this coming. He should have protected you."

She thought of all the years Franklyn Kerr had kept the secret of who her real father was. "In his own way he has." She smiled. "He sent you here."

Unable to keep from touching her, he threaded his fingers through her hair. "But who," he asked huskily, "is going to protect you from me?"

Seven

There was nothing tentative in the way his mouth took hers. His hunger was too great, his need too strong for him to be gentle with her. The sexual frustration of the last couple of days had made him a powder keg ready to explode. The thought of any harm coming to her struck a need deep inside him to keep her safe, blending with all the other powerful feelings she created in him.

Her response was immediate and total. Her arms twined around his neck, her slight weight pressed against his firm body. If desire were a color, it would be a fiery red, a flash of fire, hot and intense. They were near the edge of the blaze, near the edge of madness as his tongue melded with hers.

"Joanna," he said when he tore his mouth from hers. "You taste like no one else."

She didn't want words. Words were empty and she wanted badly to be filled, to be needed, even if for only a little while. He wouldn't say the words she wanted to hear, so she didn't want to hear him say anything.

"Then taste me," she pleaded. Her voice was a blending of honey and smoke, and coated his skin with awareness. "All of me."

Shuddering, he tightened his arms around her. With the last shred of his control, he warned her, "Don't say things like that, Joanna. I'm barely holding on as it is."

"Hold on to me." She covered his face with light, fleeting kisses. "Only me."

The butterfly kisses left him craving more, like a man dying of thirst allowed only a few drops of water. He laid back on the hard stone hearth, bringing her with him. His mouth took hers roughly. He savored the feel of her slender body covering his, her hips rubbing against him in an instinctive search for pleasure, for a release of the pressure building inside her.

Insanity, he thought. Her response was leading him into helpless madness. As crazy as it was considering where they were, he couldn't deny his needs any longer. He had to have her now in the drafty ruins of a Benedictine monastery.

When her thigh parted his legs and pressed against his sensitive aroused loins, he groaned and closed his eyes to absorb the torrent of need washing over him. Unable to withstand any more of this exquisite torture, he worked his hands beneath her sweater and shirt.

Joanna made a sound deep in her throat when she felt his hand sear the bare flesh of her stomach.

As his fingers slid lower, she buried her face in his neck, her hips arching into his hand, silently begging for more of his touch.

Unable to resist the intimate heat of her, Alex tore at the opening of her jeans with his free hand and shoved the fabric aside. Even through the haze of passion, he was able to resist the temptation to remove her clothes completely. He would have given anything to be able to be with her, naked flesh against naked flesh. But though the fireplace gave off some warmth, it wasn't enough to expose all of her to the cool air.

Joanna whimpered as his fingers invaded her body, and she became utterly helpless under the sensations seizing her. Joanna's hips jerked with the shock of his body easing into hers, then she fell into the maelstrom of primal pleasure as he began to move against her. Grasping his shoulders, she raised her upper body so she could see his face. She loved the fire that flashed in his glittering gray eyes when her movement brought her hips more fully against his, thrusting him even deeper inside her.

They became immersed in each other, striving for more and more pleasure, fused together by the sensual fire licking over their flesh and through their bodies. Consumed and consuming, they were lost in each other.

He held her slender hips, helping her when she tired, his fingers pressing into her flesh, bringing them nearer the edge of satisfaction.

Suddenly they were swallowed up together in a violent whirlpool of pleasure, and they fell into the swirling sensations waiting for them.

Exhausted, stunned, and oddly peaceful, they remained locked together as the world righted itself once again.

Love swelled within Joanna until she thought she would burst with it, but she had to hold it inside. Raising her head, she looked into Alex's eyes, searching for any sign their lovemaking had meant something to him too.

There was possessiveness and physical satisfaction in the depths of his eyes as he gazed up at her. "Would you believe I didn't plan this?"

With a breathy laugh, she said, "If you had, I think you would have chosen a more comfortable place."

"It wouldn't have mattered if this was a bed of nails. I would still have made love to you." Turning his head, he saw the fire had died down a little. "You must be cold."

She smiled faintly. "Now that you mention it. . . ."

Gently separating them, he adjusted their clothing, then they sat together on the hearth. He tossed a couple more branches on the fire and slipped his arm around her to hold her close, sharing their warmth. He could feel her trembling against him and was angry at himself.

He cursed under his breath. "I'm sorry, Joanna. I should have waited."

She shook her head. Her body was quivering from the tumult of emotions still racing through her, and there was nothing she could do about it. She saw the concern in his expression and sought to reassure him.

"I have no regrets, Alex."

"I wouldn't want to hurt you, Joanna," he said soberly, almost roughly. "That's the last thing I want to do."

She knew he wasn't referring to her physical discomfort. "If I'm hurt, you'll never know about it."

He looked stricken. "Joanna, I don't—"

"I mean it, Alex. I won't play those kinds of games with you."

He sighed heavily and murmured more to himself than her, "I don't know what this is, but it's no game."

Her smile held traces of sadness she wasn't able to hide. "When you do know what it is, let me know." Looking away, she gazed at the broken stone wall. "I hope there aren't any ghosts of Benedictine nuns inhabiting these ruins. We'll have shocked them out of their habits."

He brushed a lock of damp hair off her neck. "You don't seem too shocked."

She looked at him. "Do you think I should be?"

"I don't know how you feel unless you tell me."

"I knew what I was doing, Alex. I wanted you and you wanted me. The place may be a little unusual and uncomfortable, but not what happened between us."

He studied her face for a moment. "I think making love with a man you've known for only a short time is unusual for you."

She grimaced. "That's true enough."

"So why did you?"

"I thought that was obvious," she replied a little sharply. She reached for her bag and removed the flask of tea. "I brought a sandwich with me, and Stella packed some tea. I'll share them with you."

Alex saw her hand shake slightly as she poured tea into the plastic cup. She wasn't as calm as she was pretending to be.

He shook his head. "I don't want anything right now." He wanted her, but that wasn't what she was offering. He dropped his arm from around her. "I talked to your father last night. I told him Canfield was beginning to crowd you. Your father wants to pull you out of it."

"What did you tell him?"

"I said I thought we should leave it up to you."

Stalling, she took a sip of the steaming sweet tea. "I want to help if I can."

"We don't know what will happen once you get in touch with Travis, Joanna. You could be putting yourself in danger."

"Travis wouldn't hurt me."

A hint of irritation entered his voice. "You don't know that. We know he's hired Canfield. He could have others working for him. If his plans don't turn out the way he wants, he could take it out on you."

"I can't imagine Travis hurting me physically."

Her answers were beginning to annoy him. "There's nothing stopping him from having Canfield or someone else do it for him."

"What would that accomplish?" she asked quietly. "In the past, any damage he's been responsible for has been to material possessions. A smashed-up car, a tape deck, throwing eggs at a teacher's house. Not once has he hurt anyone physically."

Alex stood up and stalked away from her, anger stiffening his spine. After several paces he turned back to face her, fury darkening his eyes. "You admitted you don't really know Travis, even though he's your brother. You don't know how he's going to react to any given situation."

"Neither do you."

"Dammit, Joanna, I don't want you to be hurt."

"Alex, I have to try. This is my family. I have to do what I can to get this mess straightened out. If one of your brothers was in trouble, you would do everything possible to help him. Travis may not be like Wally in *Leave it to Beaver*, but he's the only brother I have."

Alex stared down at her, seeing the vulnerability in the slump of her shoulders and the shadows in her eyes. A surge of tenderness coiled tightly around his heart.

At that moment he realized he loved her.

Shock ran through him like a lightning bolt. He suddenly needed to be alone to come to terms with his feelings. "We'll talk about this later. I have to get back to the house. The trees are going to be delivered, and I should be there."

He turned and disappeared around the wall of the ruins.

Joanna felt chilled. She tightened her fingers around the cup, but the chill was deep inside her. Staring down into the milky drink, she wondered what she was going to do now. She had meant what she said when she told Alex he wouldn't know if he hurt her, but she wasn't sure how well she was going to deal with the pain herself.

They had just shared the most intimate experience between a man and a woman. Apparently it hadn't meant the same thing to Alex that it had meant to her. He had belonged to her for a brief time, and she was going to have to learn to live with only having the crumbs, not the whole cake.

She didn't return to the house until she was sure her grandmother would be at her meeting. A large truck was parked to one side of the lane by the gate near the back garden. Several young trees, their roots wrapped in burlap, were in the back of the truck, along with several gardening tools. Traces of dirt on the flatbed indicated other trees had been placed there. There was no sign of the driver or Alex.

After returning the flask to the kitchen, she went directly up to her room, thankful she hadn't run into Stella. As soon as she entered her bedroom, she walked over to the window. Gazing down at the orchard, she saw Alex immediately, as well as three other men. Instead of leaving the job of digging the holes to the men from the nursery, Alex was working alongside them. Actually, it looked like he was doing most of the work. Watching him lifting a shovel full of rich black dirt, she wondered if he was assisting because he wanted to or to hurry the job along.

Leaving the window, she took her robe out of the wardrobe and went into the bathroom. She remained in the shower for ten minutes, letting the hot water sluice over her. Back in her bedroom, she laid down on the bed and fell asleep almost immediately.

Hours later, she was vaguely aware of the sound of water running. Her sleep-fogged mind decided it was raining again. Rolling over, she was lulled by the steady cadence of water and fell back into a sound sleep.

After his shower, Alex went into her bedroom instead of his own. One towel was wrapped around his hips and another was draped around his neck. He stared at her lying on her side, one long leg exposed by her robe gaping open.

She was his. A heavy weight seemed to have been lifted off him once he had gotten over the shock of realizing how he felt about her. He loved her and she was his. Even more amazing, he was hers. Heart, body, and soul.

Whether she liked it or not, he was firmly entrenched in her life, and whatever affected her was his business. He had rushed her at the ruins, but now he would take his time for her to learn to trust him. And, he hoped, to love him.

He walked slowly to the foot of the bed and touched her ankle, shaking it enough to arouse her, not trusting himself to touch her anywhere else.

Joanna frowned, and she sighed deeply as she was jostled again. Rolling onto her back, she slowly opened her eyes. Looking down at her feet, she saw the hand on her ankle and followed the arm attached to it until she discovered who was awakening her.

"Wake up, sleepyhead. You have a little under an hour to get ready."

She had expected him to be distant or cold when she saw him again, but he was smiling warmly at her without any trace of remoteness in either his eyes or his voice. Whatever the reason for his sudden departure at the ruins, it seemed to have magically disappeared.

"What time is it?" she asked huskily, her tongue thick with sleep.

"It's a little after six. You missed tea with your grandmother, but I explained your stroll in the country wore you out." His smile deepened. "Don't worry. I didn't tell her how her granddaughter seduced me among the ruins."

"I did no such thing," she said indignantly.

"I didn't mind, darling, but I think your grandmother would."

She threw a pillow at him, and it landed with a satisfying thud against his bare chest.

Grinning, he gave her foot one last pat and walked over to the wardrobe to sort through her clothes. "Our reservation's for seven, so you'd better get dressed. Your grandmother wants us to have a drink with her before we leave. We have a busy night ahead of us."

More awake now, she propped herself up on an elbow and looked keenly at him. He seemed perfectly at home in her bedroom dressed only in a towel, and the tension she had seen in his eyes at the ruins was absent.

She should be relieved but his turnaround was confusing, and she didn't know what to make of it.

"Digging in the dirt seems to agree with you," she said dryly. "Did you happen to strike oil when you were planting the apple trees?"

He took a white dress from the wardrobe and laid it over the foot of the bed. "No such luck. I did find something more important than oil, though." His fingers trailed over the silky dress, as he imagined her wearing it and him running his hands over her. "I might even tell you what I discovered later after dinner. That is, of course, if we ever get there."

Taking the less than subtle hint, Joanna threw her legs over the side of the bed and sat up. She glanced at his scanty attire. "I'm not the only one who has to get dressed. Unless you plan to go to the restaurant like that."

"Stella wouldn't like it. I'll change into something even she will approve of. I would be a gentleman and offer you the use of the bathroom first, but we're running out of time. We'll have to share."

Joanna blinked. Maybe sharing a bathroom with a member of the opposite sex was something he was used to, but she wasn't. Then she lifted her chin. If he could do it, so could she.

While he spread lather over his jaw and shaved, she applied her makeup, amazed at how natural it was to be with him, sharing the only mirror in the bathroom.

Eventually he wiped the remaining lather off his jaw and stepped back to give her more room.

She could feel his gaze on her and met his eyes in the mirror. Her breath caught in her throat at his intent stare.

"Why are you looking at me that way?"

Something flickered in his eyes. "It was a mistake to make love to you."

She flinched as though he had struck her, and glanced away from him. A hard hand clamped onto her shoulders and turned her around, yet she wouldn't lift her head. She struggled to get free, but he wouldn't let go of her.

Realizing too late how she had interpreted his words, he held her tightly. "Joanna, I didn't mean that the way it came out. I meant it was a mistake to make love to you because now that I know what it's like to have you, I want you even more than I did before."

She stopped trying to get away from him and slowly raised her head. She searched his eyes. Then she retreated into herself, afraid of revealing her feelings.

Pain clutched at him. She had said he wouldn't know if he hurt her, but she had been wrong. He did know.

Gathering her into his arms, he simply held her, letting his nearness give her the comfort she needed, giving her his strength and warmth. Her vulnerability surprised him, and he hurt because she was hurting. So many things about her surprised and intrigued him. She wasn't as tough as she wanted him to think she was.

Oddly enough, the fact that he could hurt her gave him the confidence he so badly needed. In order to be hurt, she had to care.

When he felt her relax and rest more heavily against him, he said softly, "We have a lot to learn about each other."

Her self-conscious laugh came out as a mere breath of a sound. "You've just learned I'm a sensitive fool."

Lifting her chin, he looked into her eyes. "No, you're not. I've been clumsy and hurt you. I promise I won't hurt you again."

He kissed her lingeringly, holding himself back from taking her mouth as deeply as he wanted. Her delicate hands stroked his chest, then slid up his shoulders, bringing her breasts against the sensitized skin she had just caressed.

Finding the opening of her robe, he pushed away the barrier of cloth. He almost cried out at the painful pleasure of having her bare breasts crushed against his chest. His hands were hungrily sliding over her back and hips, and he moaned as he let his tongue imitate the movements he wasn't allowing his loins.

He was sliding dangerously into the dark void where passion ruled. Yet when he felt her fingers loosening the towel around his hips, he groaned rawly, "No!"

Joanna couldn't stop her own cry of protest.

Perspiration glistened on his skin as he loosened his passionate grip on her. Gazing into her dazed eyes, he cupped her face, his hands shaking with the need searing his blood.

"This is your grandmother's house, Joanna. I won't shame her or you by making love to you in her home without having a ring on your finger first."

Joanna couldn't breathe. Hope took the place of air in her lungs as she wondered if he actually meant to put a ring on her finger. Then reality replaced hope, and she took a deep breath to steady her rioting thoughts. She wasn't going to assume anything this time. His chivalry was rather touching, his respect for her grandmother's sensibilities commendable, but he hadn't mentioned marriage.

Visibly struggling for control, he tortured himself a last time by letting his lips close over first one breast, then the other, before pulling the edges of her robe back together and blocking out the temptation of her naked body.

He rested his forehead against hers. "Get dressed,"

he ordered, then softened the command by adding, "Please. While I can still let you go."

She started toward her bedroom when he said her name. She looked back, and he said, "When this business with Travis is over, there will be time for us. I promise."

She searched his eyes for a long moment, unsure exactly what he was promising. Then she nodded briefly and left the bathroom.

Once she was dressed, Joanna didn't wait for Alex before going downstairs. She needed the breathing space of a few minutes alone. Too much had happened in such a short time. She was venturing into an unknown territory and she had nothing to guide her other than her own instincts.

The silk dress Alex had taken out of the wardrobe was the only garment she had packed that was suitable for the occasion. It had a wraparound front with buttons from waist to hem along one side. Tiny crystal beads decorated the collar, lending an elegance to the simple design. A light filmy shawl was draped over her arm as she walked into the drawing room.

Elizabeth was already there, and immediately asked Joanna about her day as Joanna poured them each a glass of sherry. Elizabeth was pleased to hear her granddaughter had spent part of the day with Alex, and was even more delighted she was dining out with Alex. When Alex joined them, she asked him about the new apple trees, and they talked about the orchard until it was time for Alex and Joanna to leave.

As Joanna kissed her grandmother's cheek, she

saw the pleasure in the older woman's eyes and couldn't blame her for feeling satisfied with her matchmaking efforts. She had been more successful than she could ever imagine.

Their table wasn't quite ready when they arrived, so they had a drink in the lounge while they waited. They sat in upholstered chairs near the large antique waterwheel. It turned slowly through the stream that ran through the restaurant.

Alex saw Joanna glance toward the doorway. "Canfield hasn't come in yet, but he did follow us."

She frowned. Alex was seated with his back toward the entrance. "How do you know he hasn't come in?"

"There's a large framed print on the wall behind you. I can see the entrance reflected in the glass."

"And how do you know he followed us?"

"He's not very good at tailing people. He picked us up when we turned onto High Street and stayed only one car length behind us." He glanced at the creaking wheel, watching the water slide off each paddle as the wheel revolved. Shaking his head in bemusement, he murmured, "I thought I'd seen everything."

She smiled. "Are you admitting England has something Texas doesn't have?"

"If Texas has anything like this, I bet it's bigger and better," he drawled.

"Naturally," she said dryly. "This isn't your first trip to England, is it? You've been here before."

Canfield entered the restaurant at that moment. Alex wanted Joanna to remain natural so Canfield wouldn't be warned ahead of time they knew he was following them. He gave no indication he'd seen

Canfield, and said mildly, "A couple of times. I was telling you the truth about the buying trip. There are a number of orchid growers in Texas who have extensive collections and are always interested in more."

"Bigger and better?" she teased.

"Of course." Using his peripheral vision, Alex could see Canfield standing at the end of the bar at the opposite side of the room.

"But orchids weren't the only reason you've been in England before, were they? You have contacts who don't have anything to do with nursery stock. The car you've rented is from a London firm that isn't listed in tourist brochures. I noticed the leasing company's name above the license plate. Also, you knew to ask my grandmother for the telephone code, which means you know you have to have the number of the area you're calling from, not the area code of the place you're calling."

Admiration glimmered in his eyes, but he didn't give her the satisfaction of knowing her deductions had been correct. He shrugged casually. "I'm very adaptable." In an attempt to channel her thoughts in another direction, he added, "I think I proved that earlier at the ruins."

If he expected her to be embarrassed, she surprised him. Laughing softly, she met his gaze and copied his drawl. "You should be thankful old Buckaroo bucked you off so many times. Gave you a tough hide."

He nearly choked on his drink and coughed several times. As he was recovering, the maitre d' approached and told them their table was ready. Since Alex was occupied with catching his breath, Joanna smiled at the formally dressed man, who was glancing at Alex with some concern.

"He will be quite all right," she said, imitating her grandmother's formal English accent. "He's from Texas, you see," she added, as though that explained everything.

Alex was disconcerted to see that as far as the maitre d' was concerned, Joanna's explanation made perfect sense.

Their table was in a semi-private section of the dining area, exactly what Alex wanted. The single candle in the middle of the table gave Joanna's skin a shimmering glow. He let his gaze flow over her face as she read her menu. Whether there was daylight, candlelight, or darkness, she was beautiful in a way that tightened his chest and hardened his body. She was so many women all wrapped up into one, and he only hoped he lived a good long time in order to be able to become intimately acquainted with each of them.

Lowering the menu, Joanna looked up. Her breath caught in her throat at the intensity in his eyes. "What's wrong? Can't you find anything you want?"

His voice was low and slightly rough. "It's not on the menu."

Again, she surprised him. "Yes, it is," she said softly. "It has been since the day we met."

The need to touch her was stronger than ever. "When this business with Travis is over, I want you to come away with me. To a place where we can be alone."

"For how long?"

"For as long as it takes."

A waiter came up to their table at that time, and

Joanna wasn't able to ask Alex what he meant. It was difficult to maintain a normal manner in front of the waiter, yet somehow she managed to give him her order. She examined her options regarding Alex, and realized she really didn't have any. She would grasp whatever time he gave her. If that meant she was like a beggar at his door, then that's what she would have to be, taking whatever crumbs he handed out for however long he dispensed them. For a woman who prided herself on her independence, it was a galling thing to admit, but there it was.

After they had eaten and the waiter had removed their dishes, Alex drank the last of his champagne and dropped his napkin on the table. "When I leave the table," he said in a low voice, "you stay put. Let Canfield come to you."

His chair scraped loudly against the wooden floor as he pushed it away from the table. When he stood up, he stumbled and gave her a sickly smile. "I'll be right back," he said, his slurred voice louder than necessary. "I have to go to the throne room."

Joanna brought her napkin up to her lips to cover her grin, and turned her laugh into a cough as Alex weaved away from their table. She had watched in fascination each time he had poured champagne into his glass and pretended to drink. Actually, most of the champagne had ended up in the silver ice bucket the waiter had placed beside his chair. It was a waste of good champagne, but necessary in order to give the impression Alex was inebriated.

And, she told herself, if his plan was going to work, she would have to do her part. Controlling her features, she attempted to look disapproving and slightly embarrassed in case Canfield was watching.

She didn't have to wonder long if Canfield saw Alex stagger away. When he slid onto the chair, she pretended to be surprised, then changed her expression to one of irritation.

He held up his hand to ward off any protests she looked ready to make. "Take it easy. I only want to talk to you for a minute."

"I'm with someone else, Mr. Canfield. He'll be back any time."

"I saw him head for the can. It'll take him a while to find his way back in the condition he's in." He took an envelope out of his coat pocket and slid it across the table. "This is an important message from your brother. It's for your eyes only, so don't go showing it to the guy you're with."

"Why not?" she asked, hoping she had the proper note of annoyance in her voice. "What could Travis possibly write to me that someone else couldn't see?"

Canfield glared at her. "Just don't show it to anybody if you know what's good for you. You've made me wait around long enough, and time is running out. Just do what the note says, and there won't be any trouble."

She started to open the envelope, but Canfield stopped her. "Not now. I told you. No one else is to see what's in the envelope."

She slipped it into her purse, relieved when he sat back in the chair. It wasn't that she was afraid of him. She just didn't like him near her. She noticed he kept glancing in the direction Alex had gone, clearly not eager to have the other man find him there. It was obvious that drunk or sober, Alex wasn't the type of man Canfield wanted to confront.

In an attempt to get whatever information she

could, she asked, "Why couldn't Travis come himself if he wanted to contact me?"

Canfield's eyes narrowed. "He's tried to call the house several times, but someone else always answered the phone."

"He could have left a message for me to call him back," she answered in a reasonable tone, hoping she gave him the impression she wasn't aware of any trouble her brother might be in.

"Travis said you would help him. He'd better be right. You do what the note says and you won't get hurt."

He left as abruptly as he had arrived, leaving his threat hanging in the air.

Eight

If Canfield thought his parting remark would scare Joanna into doing what he said, he wasn't as clever as he thought he was. It made her darn mad.

When Alex returned to the table and nearly missed his chair as he tried to sit down, her face was a picture of fury. Anyone watching her would think she was upset because of his drunken condition, but Alex knew better. He had found a spot where he could watch the table during the whole time Canfield was with her. From his vantage point, he couldn't hear what was being said, but he could tell when Joanna became angry.

He was amazed he understood what she was thinking and feeling, even though her expression gave nothing away. It was as if he was on the same wavelength, able to discern more than anyone else could about her. Somehow that thought was more intimate than what had happened between them at the Abbey.

Because Canfield hadn't left the restaurant after delivering his message, Alex had to keep up the drunken act. As they went out the door, Joanna put her arm around his waist, and he flung his over her shoulders, as though he needed help walking. She loudly ordered him to give her his car keys for the benefit of the couple exiting behind them.

"Aren't you carrying this a little too far?" he mumbled under his breath. "I'm not really drunk."

"If Canfield follows us back to my grandmother's, he will think it's strange if you suddenly become stone sober." When he still hesitated, she said with amusement, "To make this more realistic, I should search your pockets for the keys and take them away from you."

She felt his arm tighten around her shoulders. "I don't recommend it. You might get more than you bargained for."

Still maintaining his role as a drunk, he handed over the keys and clumsily got into the passenger side of the car. As soon as Joanna slid behind the wheel, he reached for her.

His kiss was anything but clumsy as he captured her mouth. The anger Canfield had roused in her disappeared like smoke in a strong wind the second his lips covered hers.

All too soon, he lifted his head and slanted a glance toward the restaurant. Canfield stood under the lighted entrance, staring at the Jaguar, then headed for his car.

"He must have got his training from Spies R Us," Alex muttered.

She chuckled. "He's really not very good at it, is he?"

"What did he say to you? I couldn't see if your toe was tapping, but I could feel you bristling clear across the restaurant."

It didn't take her long to describe the brief meeting with Travis's messenger, though she left out the threat. She took the unopened envelope out of her purse.

He didn't want it. "Keep it until we get to the house."

He knew the information in the envelope was why he had come to England, why he had arranged to meet Joanna in the first place, but at the moment, it was the last thing on his mind.

Her scent drifted around him, filling his senses with grinding desire. He let the tips of his fingers trail along the side of her face, his thumb stroking across her moist bottom lip. There was enough light coming from the entrance of the restaurant and a single streetlamp so he could see the desire warming her eyes.

Her voice came like a soft breeze across the small space between them. "Is this for Canfield's benefit? To make him think you're trying to get back into my good graces?"

"This is for me," he murmured. He stroked his hand down her throat and over the curve of her breast, torturing himself with the tantalizing shape under his fingers. He could see the yearning in her eyes, feel her breath quicken against his skin. "When I came into the drawing room tonight, I wanted to do this."

Her voice was low and husky with need. "When you came into the drawing room, I wanted you to do this." She took his hand and slid it through the opening of her dress. His touch seared her skin as she pressed his hand against her bare breast.

He groaned and shut his eyes for a moment as desire stabbed through him. "Joanna," he said urgently, "If I'd known you weren't wearing anything under that dress, I would have had to touch you, whether your grandmother was in the room or not."

She trembled as he caressed her breast, her breath ragged against his neck. Needs grew, excitement pulsed in her bloodstream, desire streamed through her. The gearshift on the console between their seats became a frustrating barrier, and she muttered a complaint when she was unable to move closer to him.

Reluctantly, Alex withdrew his hand from the front of her dress and gently pressed her back behind the wheel. He wanted her then, that second, and figured it was a good thing they were in the car in a public car park. Otherwise he would have given in to the hunger she created so easily within him.

"We'd better go," he said quietly. "One of these days we're going to find a bed and never leave it for at least a week." He took a deep breath. "Do you still want to drive home?"

Nodding, Joanna turned the key, not surprised to see her hand shaking. It was a good thing she was accustomed to driving in England, she thought, or she would have had them in a ditch during the three-mile drive back to Chesham. Her mind was solely on the man sitting beside her, not the road or the other cars. It was rather frightening how he could take over every other thought or concern in her mind.

When they arrived, the house was quiet. "My grandmother must have had an early night."

Alex closed the front door and locked it behind them. "Hopefully Stella has too. Do you think we would be committing a mortal sin if we made a pot of coffee in her kitchen?"

"I'll do it." She took the envelope out of her purse and handed it to him. "Here. You read this while I'm making some coffee. I'll bring it into the library."

He saw the envelope was still sealed. "You haven't read it?"

"There hasn't been time. You can tell me what it says when I come back with the coffee."

Her automatic trust warmed him. He watched her as she walked down the hallway. She kept surprising him. She amazed him. She drove him crazy. She was the most fascinating woman he had ever known. And loving her scared him more than being at the wrong end of a gun.

He ripped open the envelope as he walked toward the library. This message from Travis better be what they had been waiting for all this time. He wanted this whole damn thing over so he and Joanna could put it in the past.

He was seated behind the desk with a sheet of buff-colored paper held in one hand and the phone receiver in the other when she brought a tray of coffee into the library. She set the tray down on the corner of the desk and poured their coffee, placing his in front of him. Taking her cup and saucer with her, she sat down in one of the chairs near the desk, kicking off her shoes and curling her legs underneath her.

Alex tossed the paper onto the desk and finished the instructions he was giving to Richard Sanders. "As soon as you get the address, call me back here."

He listened for a minute, then said, "My apologies to the lady, but this has to be done right away." After another short pause, he grinned and replied, "Same to you."

When he replaced the receiver, he was still smiling. "I interrupted his plans for the evening with a member of the fairer sex."

"You interrupted whose evening?"

"One of my contacts in London. He's tracking down the address to go with the phone number your brother wants you to call. Hopefully Travis is at that number, and we'll know where he is."

Shades of James Bond, she thought. "Why don't I just call the number? Maybe he'll tell me where he is."

Alex pushed the phone across the desk to her. "When you talk to him, let him think you haven't the faintest idea what's going on. Let him do all the talking. If he wants you to meet him somewhere, stall him. Tell him it will take you time to make the arrangements."

"Maybe you'd better make the call yourself," she said with irritation as she picked up Travis's note.

There wasn't much to read. Travis had written down a phone number in Seattle with blunt instructions not to give the number to anyone under any circumstances. " 'Don't tell anyone if you know what's good for you,' " she read aloud. Raising her eyes to meet Alex's, she said with amusement, "That's a line he used when he was about eight years old."

Alex didn't think it was funny. "His threats may not be original, but that doesn't mean he won't carry them out."

Joanna stared at him for a minute with a puzzled

frown. "Travis has never impressed me as being a particularly tough individual. He may have complained loudly, but he always did as he was told. I can't remember one time he ever stood up to my father, at least to his face. Travis's acts of rebellion were against things, not people."

Somehow he needed to persuade Joanna to take Travis's warning seriously. "Any man who steals from the government has to know the penalties and be willing to risk his freedom. That can make a man exceedingly dangerous."

Joanna looked back at the paper in her hand, reading it again. Without waiting for any further instructions from Alex, she made the phone call.

Five minutes later, she plunked the receiver down. Apart from saying hello, she hadn't said another word. She'd listened, jotted down a number on the paper, then hung up.

Alex was frowning at her. "When I said to let him do all the talking, I didn't mean you weren't supposed to say anything at all."

"He's smarter than you thought. I reached an answering machine."

That was something Alex hadn't expected. "What was the message?"

"I'm to pick up a specified amount of money from my father in Washington and go on to Seattle. Then I'm to call a number he gave me before I leave the money under a certain table in the restaurant at the top of the Space Needle. Once he gets the money, the missing microchip will be delivered to me at my apartment." She stood up and put her cup and saucer back on the tray. "It looks like I'll be leaving England sooner than I thought."

Alex had been about to take the sheet of paper with the new phone number from her, but stopped when he realized what she meant. "You aren't going anywhere."

"Of course I am. I just told you. I'm to deliver the ransom money so the microchip will be returned. That's what this is all about, remember?"

He stood abruptly and came around the desk to her. "You're staying right here until this is all over."

"Alex," she said patiently, "Travis expects to hear my voice when I call that number. He could also be watching the Space Needle when the delivery is made. I have to do it myself. You know that."

"You aren't going, Joanna."

His autocratic manner was beginning to annoy her. Without her realizing it, her toe began to tap against the floor. "Give me one good reason why not."

The muted sound of dogs barking and a door closing at the other end of the house filtered through to them. Stella was letting the dogs in for the night.

Joanna let out a startled gasp when Alex suddenly picked her up and carried her out of the library.

"Alex! Are you crazy? Put me down."

"If I'm crazy, it's all your fault."

Carrying her easily, he went out through the side door and took long strides across the wet grass in the back garden. His determination to get her alone was overpowering. He strode up the steps to the gazebo and let her body slide down his until she was standing in front of him, his hands clamped on her waist.

He lowered his head until his mouth was only an inch from hers. "This is the reason I don't want you to go to Seattle."

Driven by desire, fear, and love, he pulled her into his arms and kissed her fiercely. His hands were all over her, stroking, pressing, caressing. He was a man possessed, a man obsessed by the woman in his arms.

Tearing his mouth away from hers, he touched his lips to the pulse beating madly in her throat. "I couldn't take it if you were in danger, Joanna."

She could feel the tension in his body, pressed so tightly against hers, in the viselike grip of his hands. She could hear it in his voice. "I told you. Travis wouldn't hurt me."

"You were surprised he would steal anything in the first place. You don't know him as well as you think you do. You don't know what he's capable of doing to you or anyone else. I don't want you to find out the hard way."

She touched his face to soften the impact of her words. "I have to go, Alex."

The professional in him knew she was right, but emotionally he fought against the idea. To stop them from arguing, he kissed her.

Blending with his violent need to feel her velvet heat surround him, he felt a fierce desire to keep her safe. He unbuttoned her dress and spread the skirt open so he could caress her bare skin. With his hands at her waist, he lifted her effortlessly, and his mouth closed over her naked breast. Her skin was hot against his lips, and his tongue moistened and teased her hard nipple.

She shuddered helplessly under the assault to her senses, her hands gripping his shoulders as she arched her back to seek more wrenching pleasure. Even though the evening air was cool, she was burning up with the flames of passion he was stoking within her with the intimate touch of his tongue and lips.

He lowered her onto a cushioned bench. A wisp of silk was the only barrier to his possession, and he ran the tip of a finger along the lace edge across her stomach.

The way she spoke his name in a soft, husky whisper was almost his undoing. Knowing she wanted him was headier than any fine wine.

His eyes never left her as he stood and tore off his clothes. She watched him without making any effort to cover herself, her gaze trailing over him.

Her mouth curved into a soft smile. "I never thought a man could be so beautiful."

Her words rocked him almost as much as the approval and lack of fear he saw in her eyes. "The way you make me feel is beautiful," he said hoarsely.

By lifting her arms toward him, she invited him to be beautiful with her. Somehow, he remembered to take precautions to protect her before he came down over her, his legs tangling with hers. The impact of feeling her satin skin against his was like searing lightning, and he felt the storm building within him.

"I want to touch every inch of you but I can't wait. I have to have you now."

She responded by parting her legs. She brought her arms up around his back and lifted her head to offer her mouth as well as her body.

He moved partially away from her to remove the last obstacle, and she made a soft sound of protest when he lifted his weight from her.

"I'll be back," he said softly. "I'm not going anywhere."

His fingers slipped under the lace and he slid the delicate silk down her legs. As he brought his body back over hers, a soft sigh brushed against his lips, and he lowered his head to take her mouth.

His calloused hands skimmed over her ribs, her waist, the slender curve of her hip before returning to her breasts. His fingers teased and tormented the hard buds, preparing them for his mouth. As she breathed his name, her hands dug into his back, urging him to put an end to the ache inside her.

"Alex, please," she begged softly. "I need you. Now. Inside me. Please."

Her words were like claws ripping apart his control. Gently, using every last ounce of control left in him, he eased into her. He closed his eyes as white-hot sensations blazed along his spine, and she arched her hips to meet his, engulfing him completely.

Time and place became unimportant. They were hurled into the dark cavern of sensual secrets they shared together. Potent sensations poured over them, and they moved frantically together to find the pleasure waiting for them, their voices blending with the darkness when they found it.

After a long, long moment, Alex became aware of the chilly air, and felt a stab of remorse for taking her with so little regard for her comfort. Again. As it had at the ruins, the need to bury himself deep inside her had overcome any other consideration. He wondered if the desperate need for her would ever ease.

Without being aware of it, he had removed her dress completely. It was on the floor along with their other clothing. He grabbed his suit coat, then rolled onto his back, bringing her with him, unable to leave her body just yet. He spread his coat over her back before sliding his arms around her.

Joanna buried her face in his neck and sighed heavily. His scent filled her as she pressed her lips against his throat. His heartbeat still pulsed faster than normal, echoing the throbbing of her own. If she could be granted three wishes by a genie, she thought, they would all be to remain exactly where she was forever.

Her sensitive flesh felt the subtle reflexive motion of his body inside hers, and she raised her head to look down at him. The sensual expression in his eyes stunned her. She thought she saw something more, and softly uttered his name, her voice cracking with emotion.

He smiled as he met her eyes. "I know," he said huskily, as though answering a question. His hands covered her bottom, bringing her into the cradle of his hips as he moved slowly inside her.

The incredible sequence began again, more frenzied than before as the wild craving devoured them. Mists of passion coated their skin and clouded their vision as they approached the edge of primal pleasure. Suddenly the world shattered around them and they fell over the edge, calling out each other's name in gut-wrenching ecstasy.

Alex couldn't relinquish his hold on her as he stared up at the ceiling. It was humbling to admit how much he needed the woman in his arms. His brothers had always been an important part of his life, but had never been as necessary to him as Joanna. Being without her would be like having to live without his heart. If anything happened to her . . .

"I'm going with you."

For a moment, she wasn't sure she had heard correctly. Pushing herself up with her hands on his shoulders, she looked down at him. "To Seattle?"

His fingers closed around her wrists to pull her hands away. His eyes closed as he absorbed the feel of her breasts against his chest. "We'll go there first."

"First?"

"I think it's time you see Houston."

She stared at him. Her heart turned over in her chest as his words registered. She wanted to believe there would be a future for them. She would never ask for anything else out of life. Thoughts of her job at the clinic, her life before meeting Alex flickered in her mind, but everything was unimportant compared to him. She hadn't had a life until Alex.

He was startled to see tears glistening in her eyes. "Why are you crying?"

"I'm not."

He caught the moisture sliding down her cheek with one finger. "What's this then?"

"Relief. I thought I was going to have to say good-bye."

He tightened his arms around her. "That's one word I never want to hear you say to me."

He thought of the words he hadn't said to her, the same words he wanted her to say to him. Did she love him? he wondered as a sliver of fear embedded itself in his chest. He had to believe she did or he would go crazy.

He could feel her shivering against him. "When I was young, I wanted so many things. A great car, tons of money, travel to exotic places, an exciting job. Now I would settle for a warm bed." He gently released her. "You'd better get your dress on before you freeze."

They dressed quickly. Alex wrapped his suit coat around her as they left the gazebo and slipped his arm around her waist, needing to feel her close to him.

Inside the house, he walked her to the stairs and gave her one last kiss. "I'll see you in the morning."

"Aren't you going to bed?"

He shook his head. "I have a few calls to make."

"All right. Good night." She went up several steps, then turned back to look down at him. He was still at the foot of the stairs watching her.

"When we get to Seattle," she said in a low voice, "I don't want to go to bed alone."

He sucked in his breath harshly, the thought of lying with her in a bed hardened his body and softened his heart. "No," he said hoarsely. "You won't go to bed alone."

Her gaze broke away from his finally, and she continued up the stairs.

After he watched her go up the stairs, Alex headed for the library, mentally figuring out the time change between England and Washington, D.C.

Nine

Alex arranged for them to fly back to the States the following afternoon. He spent the morning in London, returning his rental car and meeting with Richard Sanders to get the information he had asked for. He also requested certain precautions to be made in Seattle before they arrived.

While Alex was in London, Joanna packed and talked to her grandmother, somehow managing to explain the sudden change of plans without telling her about the trouble Travis was in. As long as Alex and Joanna were leaving together, though, Elizabeth wasn't too disappointed Joanna was cutting her visit short.

While they waited for their flight at Heathrow Airport, Alex told Joanna they would be flying directly to Seattle instead of stopping in Washington, D.C. to pick up the ransom money. Arrangements had been made for the money to be brought to her apartment.

The flight from London to Seattle took twelve hours, but because of the time changes, it was only a little after six in the evening when they finally went through customs in Seattle. By the time they arrived at Joanna's apartment, they didn't have the energy to unpack or fix something to eat. Their only priority was to shower and fall into bed.

Joanna showered first, then collapsed on her bed. She didn't even wake when Alex slid into the bed beside her and pulled her into his arms. When he encountered the silk nightshirt she wore, he grunted in disapproval. There would be other times when she would lie naked in his arms. It was a promise he made to himself before he fell asleep.

Sometime during the night, Joanna woke with a raging thirst. She slipped out of the bed to get a glass of water. When she returned to the bed, she carefully slid under the covers, trying not to wake Alex. Still, she couldn't resist moving closer to his warmth. When her leg touched his, it tangled with hers, and she felt his hand glide over her thigh to rest on her hip.

"Sorry. I didn't mean to wake you."

"I'm not awake." His voice was husky with sleep. "I'm dreaming."

His other arm slipped under her and pulled her over until she was pressed against him. "Dream with me."

He sighed as she nestled closer, pressing her breasts into his chest. He was hard and firm against her thigh, and she flexed her leg to stroke him, wanting to give him as much sweet pleasure as he was giving her as he cupped her breast.

His mouth covered hers fiercely. He swiftly unbuttoned her nightshirt and removed it so he could have her satin skin against his. His hands took advantage of the freedom of her flesh, stroking, gripping, and smoothing over her warm body.

Always before, he had led the sensual dance, but now she took over by pressing him onto his back with her hands on his shoulders. Her lips tasted and teased his salty skin, moist with desire, hot with need. Her mouth was everywhere, her hands following or leading the way over his skin.

He felt oddly helpless, yet stronger than he had ever felt before as she touched him, caressed him, kissed him, drawing from him moans of pleasure and deepened arousal. When her hand found his aching hardness and closed around him, his hips jerked against her, his body shuddering with the ecstasy of her touch.

Her mouth glazed over him like hot velvet, settling at last on his lips to explore and tantalize him. When his hand grasped her hip, she twisted away, and he groaned in frustration.

"Joanna, let me touch you. I need to feel you around me."

She brought her hips toward his hand, and he cupped her feminine heat, slipping his fingers inside her. When she ground into his hand, he felt as though he would explode with the need to be inside her, to feel her body tugging at his.

The primitive joy of knowing she wanted him as badly as he wanted her added to the pleasure he found in her. He had never felt this complete sharing before, and he knew he would never find it with anyone else but her. The need wasn't only physical, but all encompassing.

He took the control away from her by turning her on her back and slipping between her legs. His tongue entered her mouth as he surged into her, doubling the intimacy. She came apart in his arms, meeting his thrusts wildly, bringing him to the edge of his control. Her cry of ecstasy snapped something deep inside him, and he gave himself to her completely, mindlessly.

He kept her locked to him as they drifted down from the heights neither had ever reached before. Her nearness gave him peace as he rested on her body, his pulse gradually returning to normal.

Realizing he was too heavy for her, he began to separate his body from hers, but her hands pressed against his hips. "No, don't leave me yet."

"I'm crushing you."

"I don't care."

He held her hips against him as he rolled over onto his back. "I won't leave you," he murmured with more meaning than the simple words implied.

She sighed dreamily as she laid her head on his shoulder. Soon she fell into a deep sleep. Alex wanted to stay awake to revel in the feel of her softness covering him, but he was unable to stave off his body's need for rest. Even in his sleep, though, he kept her securely in his arms.

Several hours later, Alex woke again. As much as he was enjoying the delicious weight of Joanna sprawled on top of him, he knew he would be unable to go back to sleep for a while. He eased her onto the bed and kissed her, then reached for his pants. He pulled them on and quickly left the room.

Her kitchen was small and orderly. He found the canister containing coffee grounds, but it took a little longer to find the coffee maker. Once he had the coffee perking, he opened the refrigerator to see what he could fix to eat.

"Alex? What are you doing? It's four in the morning."

He glanced over his shoulder. Wearing a blue quilted robe, Joanna was leaning against the door frame, her hair mussed, her eyes sleepy.

"Did you know there are strange things growing in here?"

"I left in a hurry." She peered around him into the interior of the refrigerator. She made a face. "I see what you mean."

"I was looking for something to eat, but I think I'm looking in the wrong place."

She walked over to a cupboard and opened it. "How do you feel about pretzels, corn chips, and strawberry soda?"

"Suicidal. I was thinking more like a steak and a potato."

"Sorry. I'm all out of steak and you met one of the potatoes in the fridge."

He shut the refrigerator door and walked over to her. "If you mean one of those little brown wrinkly things, I'll pass. What's in the canisters?"

"Here." She handed him a pretzel. "There're a couple of bottles of strawberry soda under the sink."

He bit into the pretzel. "I'll skip the soda."

She helped herself to a bottle of soda and carried the pretzels with her as she headed for the doorway.

"Where are you going?"

"To bed. My feet are cold."

Since she had the only eatable food in the whole apartment, he followed her. When he entered the bedroom, she was sitting in the middle of the bed, munching on a pretzel.

He joined her. "Did I tell you your father is arriving tomorrow?" He glanced at his watch. "Or rather today?"

"No, you didn't. Is he coming here, to my apartment?"

Alex nodded. "He's bringing the money. He wants to be on hand when we find Travis." He frowned as he reached for a pretzel. "We're going to have to get some decent food, Joanna. We can't exist on stale pretzels."

She drank some strawberry soda. "Now is as good a time as any to tell you I'm not a good cook."

Her confession didn't seem to bother him. "No problem. I am."

She smiled. "Modest, aren't you?"

"Just being honest. Growing up in an all-male household forced all of us to learn to cook or go hungry."

Against his better judgment, he took the bottle of soda from her and swallowed some. Grimacing, he handed it back. "I hope you aren't real fond of this type of drink, Joanna. If you are, we've got a problem."

She looked at him, enjoying the sight of his tanned chest and the teasing glint in his eyes. "Is that the only problem we have?"

"It's the only one I can think of." His gaze drifted over her. "I take that back. There is one other problem."

Puzzled, she met his gaze. "What is it?"

He removed the pretzels from her lap and the bottle of soda from her hand, set them on the floor, then gently shoved her on her back.

He tugged at her robe. "This is a problem."

She smiled. "What's wrong with it?"

"There's too much of it."

"There's a solution to that, you know."

He kissed her eyes, her nose, and finally her mouth. "I know what my solution would be. What's yours?"

She brought her hands around to stroke his bare back. "Take off the robe."

He lowered his head and murmured against her lips, "What a coincidence. That's my solution."

Later that morning, the doorbell rang twice before the unfamiliar sound woke Alex. He struggled to focus on his watch, then was instantly awake when he remembered whom he was expecting. It required a great deal of strength for him to ease his arm out from under Joanna.

He couldn't help smiling when she grumbled incoherently before rolling over onto her stomach.

The bell pealed stridently as he reached for his pants and shrugged into his shirt. If it was who he thought it was, it wouldn't be a good idea to go to the door half-dressed.

Senator Franklyn Kerr was about to ring the bell again when Alex opened the door. Dressed in an immaculate gray suit, Joanna's father was carrying a leather briefcase. The case was handcuffed to his wrist. Lines of exhaustion creased his face.

"Come on in, Franklyn," Alex said. "I'll heat up the coffee."

"Where's Joanna?"

"She's still sleeping. As you know, it's a long flight from London. We crashed as soon as we arrived."

Stepping over the threshold, Franklyn glanced at Alex's bare feet and his shirt tail hanging down outside his pants. He was no longer a senator but a father.

"Unless I'm mistaken," he said, disapproval apparent in his voice, "there is only one bedroom in this apartment."

Alex had been about to go into the kitchen, but he stopped and faced the senator. "You aren't mistaken."

Franklyn Kerr could tackle all sorts of governmental red tape, deal with disgruntled constituents, and meet with the President with more ease than he seemed able to deal with the situation confronting him at this moment. He cleared his throat. "I don't know whether I should threaten you with a horse-whip or congratulate you. Which should it be?"

Alex had too much respect for the older man to lie to him. "I'm in love with your daughter, Franklyn. I won't hurt her." He added with a hint of warning in his voice, "And I won't let anyone else hurt her."

Franklyn studied him for a minute, then nodded. "You mentioned something about coffee."

Alex thought Franklyn looked as though he could use something stronger than coffee, but went with his original offer. He was relieved Joanna's father had accepted his involvement with her, though he knew it wouldn't have made any difference if the senator had disapproved.

A small table with two chairs sat beneath the

kitchen window. "Why don't you sit down while I get the coffee?" Alex suggested.

The senator pulled out a chair and sat down. He unlocked the handcuff around his wrist and set the case down on the floor.

Alex glanced at the case. "Joanna insists on delivering the money herself."

"You have to stop her," Franklyn said tightly.

"He's already tried," Joanna said. "I'm going."

Wearing the quilted robe once again, she walked across the kitchen and leaned down to kiss her father's cheek. "You could try to persuade me, too, if you like, although it won't do you any good."

Franklyn's expression was a mixture of pleasure and surprise as she turned to Alex and raised up on her tiptoes to touch his mouth with hers, the gesture automatic and natural.

She smiled up at Alex. "I see you've been busy this morning. Did you ask my father to try to talk me out of delivering the ransom?"

"Would it do any good?"

She laughed. "No, it wouldn't." She looked over at her father. "But I'm glad you're here, Dad."

The look of relief that crossed Franklyn's face was almost painful to see. "Are you all right?" he asked hesitantly.

"I'm fine. I'll be even better once I have a cup of coffee."

"You know what I mean," her father said emphatically.

Alex saw the concern in the older man's eyes. "Joanna," he said quietly, "your cupboards are bare. I'll go get us something to eat."

She shook her head. "You don't need to leave, Alex." She sat down at the table across from her father. "Everything is the way it was before, Dad. It took me a trip halfway around the world to finally realize that. When Travis first showed me the birth certificate, I admit I was thrown off-balance. Now I know who you are, and who I am."

The senator covered her hand with his own. "I want you to know I loved your mother. It was no sacrifice on my part to marry her. When you were born, I loved you too."

She turned her hand over to grip his. "I know. I'm sorry I didn't realize sooner that you were my father in every possible way except biologically."

"I understood how you must be feeling. I knew you needed time to come to terms with what you had learned. Unfortunately, this trouble with Travis came up and I wasn't able to take the time to help you through it."

"Even when I visited you in D.C. before I went to England, I believe I knew I had been wrong to think you had only provided for me out of a feeling of responsibility toward your wife's child."

Franklyn had to clear his throat before he could speak. "Well, I'm relieved that's settled. Alex, could we have that coffee now?"

Alex brought them the coffee, and briefly squeezed Joanna's shoulder before returning to the counter to drink the coffee he had poured for himself. She met his steady gaze, acknowledging the simple gesture as his way of saying he understood and cared.

Her father caught the silent message. "At least something good has come out of this wretched situation Travis has got himself into, although I have to admit it wasn't what I expected."

Puzzled, Joanna turned to her father. Before she

could ask what he meant, Alex took the opportunity to fill Franklyn in on what he had found out before they left London.

"I want to check out the address where the answering machine was hooked up. I doubt if Travis is there, but I might find something that will give me a lead on him. I don't want Joanna walking into any kind of trap. The more information we have before she delivers the money, the better chance we have of protecting her."

Franklyn had his own news. "I've consulted several psychologists about Travis. They have a long complicated name for his behavior, but they say it is treatable."

"What about the government's position? Will they allow him to receive psychiatric care instead of criminal proceedings?"

"If we get the microchip back. It's no longer classified, by the way. A more efficient chip has been developed already, making the one Travis stole obsolete before it was ever used. The government is cranky about having their property stolen, however, so we still need to get it back."

"If the microchip is no longer important," Joanna asked, "why is the government paying the ransom money?"

"They aren't," Franklyn said. "I am."

Alex and Joanna exchanged glances. After a moment, Alex said, "The government wouldn't pay. They just want the chip returned because it's their property. Am I right?"

"That's about it."

Joanna didn't understand. "Why are you paying for a chip the government no longer wants?"

Alex answered, "We don't know what Travis will do if the money isn't given to him. Your father doesn't want to take the chance he might do something crazy if we don't pay him."

"Crazier than what he's already done?" she asked, an eyebrow raised.

"He's sick, Joanna," her father said. His voice was serious, his eyes sad. "He's hurting. We have to make sure he doesn't harm anyone." He turned to Alex. "What else have you discovered?"

"My contacts have come up with a boat he's leased in your name. It should be checked out. The problem is we haven't found out where it's docked. He may be using it as a base, and that could complicate things if he cruises around instead of staying in one place."

Franklyn set his cup down. "I'll go with you."

"I don't think that's a good idea. This could be a trap for you as well, you know."

Franklyn nodded grimly. "I didn't believe you when you first suggested Travis was doing all this out of some twisted motive for revenge, but now I have to admit you may be right."

"You're a powerful man and he isn't. By stealing from the government, he thinks he can embarrass you and make you do what he wants. In his mind, that gives him power over you. It isn't for the money. The money is only a symbol."

Franklyn gave Alex a direct look and said firmly, "I am going with you."

Smiling, Alex looked at Joanna. "Stubbornness seems to run in the family."

"I prefer to call it determination," she replied as she got up from the table. "I'll leave you two to argue over who does what while I take a shower." At the doorway, she paused and looked back at Alex. "What does one wear to a ransom payoff?"

How he loved her, he thought as he saw the challenge in her eyes. "Wear a bright color so we can find you in a crowd. Low heels in case you have to move fast. Slacks instead of a dress." He had answered her seriously, but then he smiled. "Need any help?"

"I'll manage, thanks." She gave him a stern look. "You're going to shock my father, Alex."

The senator shook his head. "Not me. I've gone past shock."

Alex set his cup down and walked over to her. Running a finger down the side of her face, he murmured, "That must run in the family too. You don't shock easily either." He chuckled when he saw a faint tinge of color on her cheeks. Lowering his head, he touched her mouth with his. "We might be gone by the time you get dressed. Don't open the door for anyone and don't leave until we come back."

She met his eyes for a long moment. It was impossible for her to imagine Travis hurting her, but she knew Alex didn't share her feelings. "I need to go shopping this morning," she said. "Steak and potatoes, remember?"

"I want you to stay here. We'll go out to eat when your father and I get back." He grinned. "Have a pretzel if you're hungry."

She returned his smile and turned to go into her bedroom.

Four hours passed before Alex and the senator

returned to the apartment. Using the key Joanna had given him, Alex unlocked the door and stepped inside, then stopped abruptly and stared at the living room.

A table was overturned, a plant was knocked off a windowsill, and a lamp lay on its side on the floor, its shade crushed by someone's foot.

Color drained from his face as he uttered a single word. "Joanna."

Alex heard Franklyn gasp when he saw the room. Panic shot through him, and he quickly searched the apartment, hoping he was wrong. But the apartment was empty. In the bedroom, he picked up the silk nightshirt he had taken off her during the night and held it tightly in his hand. Her scent floated up to him, and his chest tightened as he thought of never being able to hold her again.

Back in the living room, he examined the signs of violence and his hands clenched into fists. "Dammit! I should have seen this coming."

Franklyn set the table upright, his movements slow and weary. "I didn't think Travis would go this far."

"If Travis harms her in any way," Alex vowed, "the world isn't a big enough place for him to hide, Franklyn. I don't care if he's your son. I'll find him and destroy him."

"We have to figure out what to do, Alex. The most important thing is to find Joanna. I don't think he'll hurt her. He's obviously going to use her as a hostage." Franklyn rubbed the back of his neck. "What I can't figure out is why. He has the money. I just checked. So why take Joanna too?"

"I think it's another way of getting to you. Let's be

glad he took the money. The homing device in the case will make it easier to find Travis and, I hope, Joanna."

Franklyn sat down heavily on the couch. "So what do we do now? This is more your field than mine."

Alex took a deep breath, forcing the panic down. He needed to think and not let his emotions get the better of him. He had to use every ounce of his knowledge and experience to come up with a solution. Joanna's life depended on it.

He carried the phone over to Franklyn. "You're going to make a few phone calls, Senator. With your clout and my contacts at the agency, we'll find Joanna before midnight if we have to tear the city apart."

Ten

Joanna flexed her fingers in an attempt to get some feeling back into them. Her wrists had been tightly bound behind her back for hours and her hands were becoming numb. She had given up trying to free herself. All she had accomplished was rubbing her wrists raw on the rough fiber of the rope.

She still found it hard to believe Travis had kidnapped her by force.

Earlier, when she heard someone unlocking her apartment door, she had thought it was Alex and her father returning. "I hope you brought some food," she had called out to them from the bedroom. "I'm starving."

"Sorry, sugar. I didn't bring any food."

The shock of hearing Travis's voice was nothing compared to the sight of him dressed all in black, as were the two hulking men with him. They looked like stock villains in a rather bad movie. She couldn't believe it when Travis directed the men to tie her up.

She hadn't gone without a fight, and had ended up with a cut lip. She'd bit one of the men as he tried to gag her, and he had hit her.

Now she was in a cabin on a boat docked at a marina, but she didn't know which one because she had been blindfolded before she was dragged out of her apartment. She hadn't seen or heard Travis since then. For all she knew, he might still be at her place. What if he was waiting for Alex and her father? She couldn't think of any reason he would have for harming Alex, but fear welled up inside her nonetheless. Her brother might take out his frustrations or whatever was motivating his strange behavior on Alex, simply because he was there.

She didn't want to think what would happen when Travis saw their father.

If she was going to get out of this, she was going to have to do it herself. She dug her nails into her palms, and was alarmed when she couldn't feel the pain. The canvas deck chair she was sitting on wobbled precariously as she struggled again with the bindings on her wrists. She was so intent on getting free, she didn't hear the cabin door open.

"Well now, Sis. Isn't this cozy?"

She jerked her head up. Dressed in white slacks and a navy shirt, Travis looked more normal than before—until she saw his eyes. The brother she thought she knew was no longer there. At least she was comforted by the fact Travis was with her and not in her apartment, waiting for her father or Alex.

He checked the ropes at her wrists. Satisfied, he stepped in front of her and put his fingers under her chin, frowning when he saw her swollen cut lip. "It's so hard to find good help," he said with mock sadness. "You might not believe this, Joanna, but I gave orders you were not to be hurt. I have no beef with you, but I will use you to get what I want."

"Travis, untie my hands. This has gone far enough."

His mouth tightened into a grim line. "You don't give the orders now, big sister. This is my show and I'm the director."

"You have the money, so why do you need me as a hostage? Why don't you just give me the microchip and go spend your money?"

"That's no fun."

"Is that what this is all about? You think this is fun?"

"I'm having a great time."

"Well, I'm not," she said with irritation. "What are you trying to prove?"

He walked over to another deck chair and sat down, casually crossing one leg over the other. "I'm not trying to prove anything. I'm making dear Daddy jump through my hoops instead of the other way around."

"He's never made you jump through any hoops except those in your own mind, Travis. He's always been fair to both of us."

"Half the time he didn't even know we were alive. Our father, excuse me, *my* father is a walking check-book. That's the extent of what he's done for us. He paid other people to take care of us, and he gave us an allowance."

What Travis said was true up to a point, but it was a narrow view of their father's care. "Why did you steal the microchip, Travis? For the money or to make Dad pay attention to you?"

He laughed. "For the fun of it. I wanted to see if I could do it." His amusement faded. "The last little chat I had with Daddy, he said I was wasting my life, that I should do something other than make a career out of attending one college after another. I decided to show him I could accomplish something."

"Stealing from the government wasn't what he had in mind," she murmured dryly. "Why did you make me come here with you? You have the money. You don't need to use me as leverage to get what you want from Dad."

"The money wasn't enough. I thought it would be, but I was wrong. He's going to have to come to me to ask me to let you go."

There were several taps on the door. Travis gave Joanna a strange smile as he stood up and went to the door. After a brief conversation with whoever was outside, he turned back to grin at Joanna. "How are your sea legs, sister dear?"

She knew she wasn't going to like the answer, but she asked the question anyway. "Why?"

"We're going on a little trip just in case your boyfriend has found out about the boat. Canfield says he's been a real pain, causing delays, never leaving your side. According to Canfield, your lover is someone to stay clear of, so I would just as soon keep him out of this part if I can. It won't hurt for Daddy to sweat for a few days." Opening the door again, he added, "Sit back and relax. Enjoy the cruise."

"Why are you keeping me tied up? I'm not a threat to you. Especially, if we're going out to sea. I won't be able to run away."

"Now, Joanna," he said cheerfully, "we have to do this right. What kind of a hostage would you be if you were allowed to wander around the boat? Besides, I rather like the idea of Daddy's little girl being helpless." He paused for an instant. "But then I keep forgetting, you aren't Daddy's little girl, are you? You're his little niece who he cares for more than his own son."

With a nasty smile, he went out the door and shut it behind him. Joanna closed her eyes and forced herself to breathe deeply. She couldn't believe it. She was actually frightened of Travis. How could he have changed so much? Had he really altered so drastically or had her perception of him changed?

She had to stay calm. She had to think of some way to get out of this mess. She looked around the cabin for something she could use to cut the ropes, but couldn't see a single thing that would help. The cabin was stripped of all but the furniture. There was only a narrow cot, a built-in vanity, and two canvas director's chairs. A framed marine print was on an inner wall and a single porthole was in another.

In the movies, there was always a broken glass, a letter opener, or a pair of scissors the hero or heroine could use to slice through their ropes, but this wasn't a movie. This was real life.

She could feel a throbbing beneath her feet as the engines turned over, and she sensed a change in the movement of the boat. They were going out to sea.

Since she couldn't see her wristwatch, she had no idea how long they had been underway. It seemed like hours. Then the motion of the boat changed and the engines stopped. She could see through the single porthole that the sky was brilliant with color as the sun began to set. She wondered if they were anchored out in the bay or had arrived at another marina.

Her arms were numb, and she was getting a cramp in her leg by the time the sunlight disappeared completely, replaced by an inky darkness. She hadn't eaten all day, and she was thirsty, but those were the least of her problems.

When the door opened, she expected to see Travis. Instead, the two men who had tied her up in her apartment came in. Without saying a word to her, one of them knelt behind her to untie her wrists while the other man stayed by the door. Hope began to grow inside her when she felt the ropes fall away, but was quashed when he didn't release her arms.

The muscles in her arms had stiffened from being in the same position for so long, and it was agony when the man moved them in front of her to retie the rope.

She cried out as excruciating pain shot up her arms.

The sound traveled across the water and sent chills down Alex's spine. He started to move forward, but was detained by a hand on his arm.

"Not yet, Alex," Franklyn said quietly. "I know how you feel, but we have to wait for everyone to get into position. We have to stick to the plan."

Alex's jaw ached from tension as he tormented himself with thoughts of what could be happening to Joanna aboard the boat tied at a pier a hundred yards away. A shudder ran through him, but he pushed the torturous images from him. He had to blank out every emotion in order to concentrate on the plan.

"How good are these men?" he asked.

"They're all from a private security firm and come highly recommended."

A red light blinked on the small black plastic box he held in his hand. "It's a go."

Figures dressed in black moved furtively toward the boat, approaching from the pier, from the boats berthed on either side, and from a rubber raft on the water. Using the homing device planted in the leather case Travis had taken, they had been able to pinpoint Travis. Once they had found the boat, it had been easy for the rescue team to get in position.

A second light winked on the box. Alex tightened his grip on the gun in his hand and boarded the boat with the senator right behind him.

No guns or force were needed. Travis was fixing himself a drink when he looked up and saw his father, along with several other men. He cordially offered drinks all around and appeared surprised when no one accepted his hospitality.

Alex wasn't interested in Travis. Ordering three men to come with him, he continued his search for Joanna.

He spotted two men coming out of a stateroom. They were quickly dispensed with. Cautiously, in case there were more men inside, Alex opened the door to the stateroom.

Joanna was lying on a cot with her bound hands tied to one of the rails in the headboard. His heart turned over when she looked up at him and smiled weakly. "Hi."

Kneeling beside her, he took a knife out of his boot and slit through the ropes.

He heard someone enter the room behind him. "Are you all right, Joanna?" Franklyn asked.

"I've been more comfortable but I'm okay."

Fury flashed through Alex when he saw the raw, bleeding skin around her wrists. Then he looked up and noticed her cut lip.

"Get Travis off this boat, Franklyn," he said in a quiet deadly voice, "before I get my hands on him, or you won't have a son."

"He's being taken off now," Franklyn said.

Alex sat on the edge of the bed and lifted Joanna into a sitting position. Tenderly, he rubbed feeling back into her arms, wincing when he heard her sharp intake of breath as her circulation began to flow steadily again.

Satisfied she could move her arms on her own, he pulled her onto his lap and simply held her, needing the reassurance of feeling her alive and warm against him.

"I'll take care of the cleanup, Alex," Franklyn said. "I'm taking Travis to a hospital for psychiatric evaluation, and I've asked that his friends be held until we can investigate the other men's involvement. You take care of Joanna."

Alex looked up and met the older man's eyes. "She's going home with me. You can reach us in Texas."

The senator raised a brow, then nodded.

The door closed quietly as her father left the cabin, and Joanna buried her face in Alex's neck. His arms were like iron cords around her, holding her so tightly she could barely breathe, but she didn't care. This was where she wanted to be. Her arms wound around his waist, and she was astonished to feel him trembling.

She raised her head enough to see his face. Her breath caught at the tormented expression in his eyes. "Alex?"

His gaze scanned her face, settling on her injured lip. A spasm of emotion twisted his mouth. He lowered his head and gently stroked her cut lip with his tongue, easing her pain and his own by the contact.

"Did Travis do this to you?" he asked hoarsely.

"No. It was one of his men." She felt his muscles tighten and said quickly, "It wasn't entirely his fault. I didn't exactly cooperate when they came to the apartment."

"Just before we boarded the boat, I heard you cry out."

"I was left tied up in that chair since they brought me here. Then they untied me and brought me over here, and it hurt when they moved my arms. How did you find me?"

"There was a homing device in the briefcase Travis took out of your apartment."

She smiled. "That was very clever of you."

"If I was so clever, you wouldn't be on this damn boat in the first place."

He lifted her in his arms and carried her into the small bathroom off the stateroom. Setting her down on the counter by the sink, he drenched a washcloth in cold water and carefully bathed her wrists. He knew they had to hurt like hell, but she didn't say a word. He rinsed the cloth, then held it against her lip.

"This needs ice."

She smiled as she pressed her hand against his wrist, moving the cloth away. "What it needs is a kiss."

Something changed in his eyes as he looked down at her. "I don't want to hurt you."

"You won't."

He touched her mouth with his, feeling her breath brush against his lips as she sighed. Dropping the cloth, he slanted his mouth over hers, letting his tongue stroke hers. When he raised his head, his eyes locked with hers.

"Joanna, if anything had happened to you—"

She touched his mouth with her fingers. "It didn't. I'm fine."

He kissed her fingers. "Joanna, I . . ."

"Yes."

He slowly brought his hands up to cup her face. "Joanna, I love you. I can't stand the thought of anything hurting you."

"Oh, Alex," she murmured.

He waited but she didn't say anything else.

"Usually," he said, "when someone says I love you, it's polite to say it back."

Remembering their first conversation, she asked, "Is that how it's done in Houston?"

He smiled. "That's how it's done everywhere."

She became serious, her voice low and husky. "Alex, I would never have made love with you if I hadn't loved you."

His arms encircled her, and they embraced for a long time. At last, Alex reluctantly released her. "Let's get off this damn boat. You need to see a doctor before we go home."

"I don't need to see a doctor. What I need is some food, a bath, and you."

He was relieved to hear the stubbornness in her voice. "You can have the bath in your apartment. I'll pick up something to eat while you're packing." He smiled, his eyes warm and sensual. "Once we get home, you can have me."

She was puzzled. "Packing? Where are we going?"

"Home. My home. In Houston."

"Did I miss something? Why are we going to Houston?"

He kissed her lightly. "Because that's where my family is, and they will want to be at the wedding. Your father will meet us there after he returns the microchip and has Travis committed or whatever. We don't have time to wait for your grandmother to fly over from England, but we'll go see her soon."

She stared at him. "Wedding? What wedding?"

"Our wedding. I'm not letting you out of my sight again. I need to have you tied to me in every way possible. I believe the custom is for two people to get married when they love each other and want to spend the rest of their lives together."

"There's also another rather quaint custom that I'm sure they've heard of even in Houston."

"What?"

"A man asks a woman to marry him before planning the wedding. Sometimes he even has a ring to go along with the proposal."

He scooped her up in his arms and carried her out of the small room. "Well, I'll be damned if I'm going to propose to you in a bathroom. You'll just have to wait until we get away from here."

Her arms wound around his neck. "I'll wait. Since

I will be getting married only once, I want to do it right starting with the proposal."

He stopped at the door. Outside the stateroom, there would be other people, including her father. This would be the last opportunity to be alone until they got to her apartment.

His eyes were full of everything he felt for her as he looked down at her. "I'd rather stop breathing than to live the rest of my life without you. Whether you agree to marry me or not, I want you with me."

She smiled softly. "I feel we were married in the Abbey ruins with the ghosts of Benedictine nuns as witnesses. The ceremony in Houston will be for the sake of our families."

She was right, he thought. He couldn't feel more tied to her now than if they had gone through ten ceremonies. Remembering her cut lip, he touched her lips only briefly with his, but she wanted more than a gentle kiss. Her hand came up behind his head to bring his mouth down on hers harder, and she parted his lips with her tongue.

Finally, after a long satisfying kiss, Alex lifted his head. "Let's go home."

She nodded. "Let's go home."

Epilogue

A year later.

Sunlight glittered off the snow as Joanna and Alex walked back to the house. Alex kept a protective arm around her waist in case she slipped on the icy ground.

"I still don't think it's a good idea for you to be out in this snow," he said.

"Alex, I'm only four months pregnant," she said patiently. "That hardly qualifies me as an invalid. I wanted to see how well Travis was adjusting to life on the ranch. He was actually mucking out the horse stalls and enjoying it."

"Didn't you believe Eric? He told you Travis is turning into a first-class cowhand."

"I don't believe it was as easy as Eric made it sound." She stopped and looked back toward the barn. "When my father first suggested having Travis paroled in your brother's custody, I wasn't sure it was such a good idea. I thought Travis needed professional help."

Alex chuckled. "He's got it. Don't forget, Eric raised most of the Tanner brood. If there's one thing he knows, other than horses, it's how to get work out of anyone who sets foot on the ranch. Even your father is put to work when he comes to visit."

"So are you." She smiled up at him. "And you both enjoy it too."

"You haven't exactly fought like a tiger whenever I've suggested we come out here."

"I admit it. I enjoy coming here too."

His arm tightened around her when she slipped on a patch of ice. "I wish you'd stayed in the house like I asked. You would be falling for two now, you know."

She stopped walking, turning and grabbing the lapels of his sheepskin coat. "All right, Mr. Tanner. Let's get this straight right now. I won't be treated like a porcelain figure for the next five months. I'm going to keep working at the clinic in Houston up until a month before the baby is born. I still plan on helping out at the nursery on the weekends. Pregnancy does not automatically take me out of the human race."

He grinned down at her, his hands closing over hers. "Bear with me, darling. This is my first baby. I can't help it if I want you and him to be safe."

"Him?"

He took her arm and drew her with him toward the house. "The Tanner track record has been fairly consistent. The chances are we'll have a boy."

"Whether it's a boy or a girl, we're going to be a real family."

Alex glanced down at his wife. This wasn't the first time she had said that, and he knew why she was so adamant about being a good parent. She didn't want her children to feel neglected or ignored like Travis had.

They had reached the steps leading to the porch of the large ranch house. Inside were various members of his family. This would be the last moment of privacy, so he took advantage of it.

He turned her to face him and cupped her face in his hands. "I once asked Eric how he knew what to do when he suddenly became responsible for all of us after my father died. His answer was he did the best he could. That's all we can do, Joanna. We may make a few mistakes, but between us we have enough love for a dozen children."

She smiled. "A dozen children? I know you come from a big family, Alex, but I hadn't planned on having a brood."

He lowered his head and kissed her, wishing they were in their own house where he could kiss her the way he wanted. "We'll negotiate the number later after we get home."

She wrapped her arms around his neck. Whatever they decided, she felt very lucky to have Alex in her life. The addition of their children made the future even more exciting and fulfilling.

"As soon as we get home," she said, "I'll get the pretzels and strawberry soda out so we can have something to snack on. I have a feeling it's going to be a long discussion."

He kissed her again, his mouth lingering on hers. "It might take all night."

THE EDITOR'S CORNER

With the very special holiday for romance lovers on the horizon, we're giving you a bouquet of half a dozen long-stemmed LOVESWEPTs next month. And we hope you'll think each of these "roses" is a perfect one of its kind.

We start with the romance of a pure white rose, **IT TAKES A THIEF**, LOVESWEPT #312, by Kay Hooper. As dreamily romantic as the old South in antebellum days, yet with all the panache of a modern-day romantic adventure film, Kay's love story is a delight . . . and yet another in her series that we've informally dubbed "Hagen Strikes Again!" Hero Dane Prescott is as enigmatic as he is handsome. A professional gambler, he would be perfectly at home on a riverboat plying the Mississippi a hundred years ago. But he is very much a man of today. And he has a vital secret . . . one he has shouldered for over a decade. Heroine Jennifer Chantry is a woman with a cause—to regain her family home, Belle Retour, lost by her father in a poker game. When these two meet, even the sultry southern air sizzles. You'll get reacquainted, too, in this story with some of the characters you've met before who revolve around that paunchy devil, Hagen—and you'll learn an intriguing thing or two about him. This fabulous story will also be published in hardcover, so be sure to ask your bookseller to reserve a collector's copy for you.

With the haunting sweetness and excitement of a blush-pink rose, **MS. FORTUNE'S MAN**, LOVESWEPT #313, by Barbara Boswell sweeps you into an emotion-packed universe. Nicole Fortune bounds into world-famous photographer Drake Austin's office and demands money for the support of his child. Drake is a rich and virile heartbreaker who is immediately stopped in his tracks by the breathtaking beauty and warmth of Nicole. The baby isn't his—and soon Nicole knows it—but he's not about to let the girl of his dreams get out of sight. That means he has

(continued)

to get involved with Nicole's eccentric family. Then the fun and the passion really begin. We think you'll find this romance a true charmer.

As dramatic as the symbol of passion, the red-red rose, **WILD HONEY**, LOVESWEPT #314, by Suzanne Forster will leave you breathless. Marc Renaud, a talented, dark, brooding film director, proves utterly irresistible to Sasha McCleod. And she proves equally irresistible to Marc, who knows he shouldn't let himself touch her. But they cannot deny what's between them, and, together, they create a fire storm of passion. Marc harbors a secret anguish; Sasha senses it, and it sears her soul, for she knows it prevents them from fully realizing their love for each other. With this romance of fierce, primitive, yet often tender emotion, we welcome Suzanne as a LOVESWEPT author and look forward to many more of her thrilling stories.

Vivid pink is the color of the rose Tami Hoag gives us in **MISMATCH**, LOVESWEPT #315. When volatile Bronwynn Prescott Pierson leaves her disloyal groom at the altar, she heads straight for Vermont and the dilapidated Victorian house that had meant a loving home to her in her childhood. The neighbor who finds her in distress just happens to be the most devastatingly handsome hunk of the decade, Wade Grayson. He's determined to protect her; she's determined to free him from his preoccupation with working night and day. Together they are enchanting . . . then her "ex" shows up, followed by a pack of news hounds, and all heck breaks loose. As always, Tami gives us a whimsical, memorable romance full of humor and stormy passion.

Sparkling like a dew-covered yellow rose, **DIAMOND IN THE ROUGH**, LOVESWEPT #316, is full of the romantic comedy typical of Doris Parmett's stories. When Detective Dan Murdoch pushes his way into Millie Gordon's car and claims she's crashed his stakeout, she knows she's in trouble with the law . . . or, rather, the

(continued)

lawman! Dan's just too virile, too attractive for his own good. When she's finally ready to admit that it's love she feels, Dan gets last-minute cold feet. Yet Millie insists he's a true hero and writes a book about him to prove it. In a surprising and thrilling climax, the lady gets her man . . . and you won't soon forget how she does it.

As delicate and exquisite as the quaint Talisman rose is Joan Elliott Pickart's contribution to your Valentine's Day reading pleasure. **RIDDLES AND RHYMES**, LOVESWEPT #317, gives us the return of wonderful Finn O'Casey and gives him a love story fit for his daring family. Finn discovers Liberty Shaw in the stacks of his favorite old bookstore . . . and he loses his heart in an instant. She is his potent fantasy come to life, and he can't believe his luck in finding her in one of his special haunts. But he is shocked to learn that the outrageous and loveable older woman who owned the bookstore has died, that Liberty is her niece, and that there is a mystery that puts his new lady in danger. In midsummer nights of sheer ecstasy Liberty and Finn find love . . . and danger. A rich and funny and exciting love story from Joan.

Have a wonderful holiday with your LOVESWEPT bouquet.

And do remember to drop us a line. We always enjoy hearing from you.

With every good wish,

Carolyn Nichols

Carolyn Nichols
Editor
LOVESWEPT
Bantam Books
666 Fifth Avenue
New York, NY 10103

THE DELANEY DYNASTY

Men and women whose loves and passions are so glorious it takes many great romance novels by three bestselling authors to tell their tempestuous stories.

THE SHAMROCK TRINITY

☐ 21786 **RAFE, THE MAVERICK**
by *Kay Hooper* — $2.75

☐ 21787 **YORK, THE RENEGADE**
by *Iris Johansen* — $2.75

☐ 21788 **BURKE, THE KINGPIN**
by *Fayrene Preston* — $2.75

THE DELANEYS OF KILLAROO

☐ 21872 **ADELAIDE, THE ENCHANTRESS**
by *Kay Hooper* — $2.75

☐ 21873 **MATILDA, THE ADVENTURESS**
by *Iris Johansen* — $2.75

☐ 21874 **SYDNEY, THE TEMPTRESS**
by *Fayrene Preston* — $2.75

☐ 26991 **THIS FIERCE SPLENDOR**
by *Iris Johansen* — $3.95

Now Available!

THE DELANEYS: *The Untamed Years*

☐ 21897 **GOLDEN FLAMES** by *Kay Hooper* — $3.50
☐ 21898 **WILD SILVER** by *Iris Johansen* — $3.50
☐ 21999 **COPPER FIRE** by *Fayrene Preston* — $3.50

NEW!

Handsome Book Covers Specially Designed To Fit Loveswept Books

Our new French Calf Vinyl book covers come in a set of three great colors— royal blue, scarlet red and kachina green.

Each 7" × 9½" book cover has two deep vertical pockets, a handy sewn-in bookmark, and is soil and scratch resistant.

To order your set, use the form below.